ICE SHACK

A NOVEL BY DAVID J. HEATH

David J. Heath

Published by Majestic Pine Publishing
PO Box 508, Two Harbors, Minnesota 55616

Printed in the United States of America

Library of Congress Control Number: 2009909750

International Standard Book Number: 978-0-9825357-0-7

Cover Design By: Dave Gilsvik

Acknowledgements

Thank you to everyone who helped me along the way. A special thanks to Donna and Theresa for all their support. This has been a long and involved project and your encouragement helped me stay focused. I have appreciated the feedback, opinions and input you have both given me.

Foreword

About the author and book:

David J. Heath is a new Minnesota novelist and holds a degree in Mass Communications from St. Cloud State University. Living in northern Minnesota, he is an avid woodsman and fisherman.

The author's knowledge of the northern boreal forest is revealed in this descriptive tale of a serial killer of nearly indestructible power lurking in the land of lakes. This individual is a true beast of the forest who knows how to live off the land and *not* just the plants and animals of the forest.

The Griffin is at the top of the food chain, and has morphed from a rebellious anti-government woodland hermit to an insane cannibal of the woods. If there ever was an animal like a Bigfoot, the Griffin is a close second.

A barely human, crazed individual who believes he is Prometheus the Griffin, a Titan from Greek mythology. He becomes the enforcer of an old Indian legend, which he believes can free him from the wrath of the gods. Rice Bay is his domain, and he learns to protect it with a brutality that puts fear into the local residents of Tanner's Lake.

The book unfolds in northern Minnesota as the frozen lake ice melts revealing the Griffin's work from the past winter….

1

The ice shack groaned and shuddered as the northeast wind blasted the plywood frame on the desolate lake. The dark figure struggled against the wind, pulling a toboggan from a shoulder harness. As the large figure dressed in animal skins approached the shelter, he swung the door open violently and dragged the toboggan inside.

Only two days before Christmas, the Thompson family was busy with the standard holiday chores. The kitchen filled the house with the aroma of freshly made chocolate chip cookies. Matt and Joe grabbed a coat pocket full of the tasty morsels as they hustled out the door with skates and hockey sticks.

"Wait for the cookies to cool," shouted their mother Jacqueline, to no avail. Actually, she was happy they had left, providing her a good opportunity to wrap some gifts. With the cold weather, they had been playing in the house for what seemed like two weeks instead of two days.

Ben Thompson pulled into the driveway after a morning of Christmas shopping. As he entered the house, he spotted his wife Jacqueline wrapping the gifts. Sneaking up behind, he wrapped his arms around her giving a playful Merry Christmas hug.

"The kids went out skating on the lake. Did you get my Christmas present?" Jacqueline asked.

"With the kids being gone, maybe I should give you a special present right now," Ben laughed, squeezing her tighter. "Or maybe I should just wrap you up and put you under the tree."

She smiled and slid away seductively. "Good things come to those who are patient. I don't want the roast to burn you know."

"With that, I think it is time to mix some cider in the thermos and go out and spear a monster northern. Almost works better than a cold shower," he laughed.

"However, when I return cold and hungry, I do expect to be overwhelmed by your beauty and warmth."

Thompson stepped into his snowmobile suit and headed out into the crisp northern air. "Fish for lunch tomorrow," he yelled, closing the storm door.

The high pressure system had finally begun to break and the outdoor thermometer read eight degrees. The snowmobile fired up easily with a turn of the key. Thompson roared out of their backyard and onto Tanner's Lake. The hockey rink was about three quarters of a mile down the lake closer to town. The sled covered the distance in less than a minute.

Thompson's dog Raven bounded up to greet the oncoming snowmobile as it approached. The boys skated over to the boards, temporarily leaving the pickup game of about a dozen kids.

"Are you going fishing?" asked Matt.

"Just until supper time. I'll pick you guys up on the way back and give you a ride, okay?"

The children acknowledged him as Thompson fired the sled back up. Spearing pike was a sport which was often productive on northern Minnesota lakes. Thompson screamed across the white expanse to a small village of ice shacks on the east side of the lake. Maneuvering around large blocks of ice cut from spear houses, he pulled up to his dark house. Positioned over a bottom ridge, it was normally a good spot this time of year. He entered the unlocked shack and grabbed his ice chisel.

A thin crust of overnight ice was broken away from the three by three square previously cut in the ice. Thompson pushed the two inch thick ice slab down below the lake's surface to get it out of the way. Then he prepared his decoy to lure in a fish, sinking it just below the ice surface.

Poised on a stool in complete blackness, he sat motionless with trident spear ready to throw. Within the dark house, a square cut in the ice was naturally illuminated from sunlight through the lake ice surface. The darker the ice shack the better for seeing the fish below the ice. That was why most of the structures were painted black. The clear water made it easy to see fish moving below, revealing an underwater world most people never experience.

The sucker minnow floated about three feet down, looking like easy prey for a large predator fish like Northern Pike and Muskellunge. Soon a large fish hovered motionless below the decoy eyeing the bait just out of spearing range. As the fish moved closer, Ben readied his spear, not noticing the dark shape directly below the fish.

The fish darted to the side as the splash of the spear pierced the water revealing the horror below. The spear struck what appeared to be the upper torso of a man floating below the surface. Thompson gasped as he pulled in the line retrieving his spear.

The distorted head popped through the ice surface with a half eaten torso filling the spear hole. The grey frozen face gazed upward with eyes open and patches of hair torn away revealing the skull. The flesh from one eye socket was rotten to the cheek bone causing the eye to hang out over the remaining facial tissue. The partial corpse sprang up a foot above the ice hole as buoyant as a cork in water. As the body bobbed up in the ice hole, it disappeared in the blackness of the dark spear house, striking him in the lower leg. Thompson dropped his spear and dove for the ice shack door smashing it open. The bright sunlight blinded him as he scrambled to his snowmobile and vomited.

Regaining his composure, Thompson jumped aboard the sled and hit the ignition. Without paying attention to the start procedure he accidentally flooded the engine. Looking around he saw no other snowmobiles parked outside the ice fishing community. The surrounding ice shacks appeared unoccupied as the wind howled across the lake.

To face reality, Thompson walked back to the ice shack and opened the door slightly to let in some light. As he peeked in, the torso lay across the hole revealing this was no hallucination.

Running back to the sled he held the throttle down and fired the engine again. This time the motor popped and he hit the throttle pointing the sled across the three mile frozen tundra toward the small resort town.

The snowmobile hit the shoreline and jumped into the park at the edge of town. Thompson ignored the no snowmobile restriction within town limits and drove the sled down the snow packed shoulder toward the Sheriff's office.

Pulling up at the front of the station, he jumped off the snowmobile and ran inside. He knew the town Sheriff, Jason Campbell, since he was a kid. One of his deputies greeted him at the door.

"Ben, you know better than to drive your sled right down the main drag."

Obviously shaken, Thompson hurried past the deputy and inside the police station.

"Where is Jason?

I just found a body in the lake," he said excitedly.

Sheriff Campbell appeared around the corner of the office.

"Slow down Ben, now what did you see?"

Thompson explained the situation. "I, I was in my spear house and saw a bod.. body.., it was horrible. I .. I..I hit it with my spear accidentally."

The officers listened to his morbid story and agreed to take a trip out on the lake. Thompson was not known to be a big drinker or a practical joker. Obviously upset, Sheriff Campbell took his story seriously. He followed him out on the lake with one of the department snowmobiles.

Upon arrival at the ice shack, Campbell pointed his flashlight inside the dark room. The beam of the light illuminated the corpse now frozen into the spearing hole. The sight shocked him and he jumped back for a second.

"Jesus, what happened to the body?" he exclaimed.

He stepped back and walked over to his sled and pulled out his cell phone. "This is Jason. We have a body out here just like Ben said. We're going to need a toboggan and a body bag to get back in what is left."

The deputies arrived in short order and were given the grisly task of gathering the corpse into the body bag and securing it on the toboggan.

The body was transported back to the local coroner's quarters just as dusk was approaching.

"Ben, can you come down to the office and give us your written statement?" asked the Sheriff.

Thompson suddenly remembered his promise to give his kids a lift home. "I need to pick up Matt and Joe at the rink first," he replied.

Sheriff Campbell offered to help run the boys home. "I'll follow you to your house and have one of my deputies pick us up in a squad car."

It was first assumed the person was probably a drowning victim from thin November ice. The strange atmosphere around the Thompson home was evident after the incident that Christmas season.

A family of fisherman living on a lake, it had always been a good fireside horror story to accidentally hook a body while fishing in the lake. Unfortunately, Ben Thompson never thought he would actually experience something of that nature.

The autopsy was performed after New Year's Day and the coroner revealed the cause of death was not from drowning. The body was that of a Hispanic woman, probably about eighteen years old. He estimated the body had been in the water for about a month. Because of the condition of the body, it was difficult to determine the exact cause of death.

One thing was certain. It was not an accidental death. The condition of the body made it quite clear this was definitely a homicide.

The skull had a large fracture in the back portion with a couple of smaller holes above it. Almost as if the holes were made from some sort of sharp object.

Only the upper torso was recovered and gender was determined by partial remaining internal organs in the pelvic regions. Oddly enough, dental database records proved worthless because all the teeth were missing.

According to the coroner's report, the condition of the body was unusual, even for a body submerged for that length of time. His report stated, the absence of teeth indicate probable physical extraction. Absence of all teeth is considered abnormal even with extensive decomposition in the jawbone region.

The case went unsolved as to the identity of the woman. Various leads on missing persons were tracked that winter with no success. The case was filed as an open unsolved murder after about three months of investigation with no leads.

The town of Jackson was located approximately one hundred miles from several larger metropolitan areas. Local investigators thought the crime was committed by someone not from the immediate area.

That winter, an occasional investigation relating to a missing person in the Twin Cities would examine the Tanners lake murder, looking for a connection.

However, nothing in the missing person database was ever tied to the case. The incident was pretty much forgotten after a few winter months passed. When the ice went out the following spring, the scope of the case was truly revealed.

Murders were rare in the small resort town of Jackson, population 2,200 people and the Jackson County seat. The last homicide was a triple murder suicide about two years ago. The probable motive in that case, was jealousy erupting from a love triangle involving out of town folk at a private lake cabin.

Town businesses relied heavily on tourism and did not discuss unsolved murders to keep up the clean, friendly fishing resort image. However, just prior to the spring fishing opener, it was obvious that something was radically wrong on Tanner's Lake. Outside law enforcement help was needed immediately.

As Lieutenant McCabe returned to his desk through the busy downtown Minneapolis FBI precinct office, his phone was ringing off the hook.

Finishing off a taco from a fast food joint, McCabe hustled to his phone, dropping meat from the sloppy hard shell over his desk as he picked up the receiver.

"Aww…Hello, this is McCabe."

The phone call was from his commanding officer, Captain Becker.

"I need to talk to you in my office, we have something major happening in Jackson County."

McCabe hung up the phone and began meandering over to the Captain's office, stopping to chat with a female co-worker on the way. Captain Becker's door swung open as McCabe approached. "Wait until you hear this one. We definitely have some work to do."

McCabe looked up and smiled, "Great, I bet this will really be a treat." Muttering, he left the attractive young woman's desk to acknowledge his boss.

Dressed in blue jeans and a flannel shirt with a shoulder holster, he walked into the Captain's office. Captain Becker looked up and opened a black notebook.

"I just got off the phone with Sheriff Campbell in Jackson County. Remember the body that turned up through the ice last winter around Christmas on Tanner's Lake?"

McCabe acknowledged.

"Sure do… that was my case. Is the Department of Natural Resources planning to set new limits on body spearing next year?"

"Bad joke McCabe. Spring thaw just broke up the ice on Tanner's Lake, and guess what?"

"The fish had been having a feast last winter. In two days they have eleven more bodies. Or should I say body parts, they are floating up under docks, tangled in anchor ropes, and washing up on shore. Who knows how many they will find before this thing is over?"

"One guy even found a bunch of gulls fighting over a headless corpse on the beach. The town folk are really upset to say the least. Kind of puts a damper on swimming and fishing with the little kiddies for next week's fishing opener, if you know what I mean."

Lieutenant McCabe's face took on a serious expression.

"Have they identified who any of them are yet?"

The Captain removed his glasses and rubbed his eyes. "I think they're all in kind of a shock right now. Sheriff Campbell told me they're bagging what they find and putting them in a cold storage facility in the morgue.

They're setting up divers and dragging operations right now. Local law enforcement agencies are assisting with extra boats and divers.

I want you to go up there and investigate the homicide situation. These are not drowning victims. It looks like we have a potential serial killer on the loose."

Captain Becker went on. "I'm sending someone from forensic with you and a small evidence team to collect anything that might be used in the case from the dragging operations. Contact me if it looks like you need any more help after you get there."

Captain Becker picked up his phone to call forensic medicine.

"I will also be scheduling a press conference to officially notify the public of what we have found so far. The press release will be at about 5:00PM, and it will probably be on national news. That is about three hours from right now. The local media is on the lake already covering the breaking story. I have a small plane and pilot ready for you at the airport. He will take you right to the Jackson airport where I will have a truck waiting for you with the usual gear in it. If you hustle, you might be on the evening news. Enjoy your flight and let me know what you think as soon as possible. Give me whatever you can before I talk to the press. Good luck."

2

Ben Thompson's guide service was not as busy as usual on opening fishing weekend. This opener, he went out with two repeat customers from a couple of years ago on his twenty two foot charter boat.

The Cadwell brothers, Mike and Jim, liked to get together every fishing opener as their tradition. This year they rented a cabin for the entire week and expectations of good fishing ran high.

Their destination was twenty one miles down the lake to the entrance of the Kawishiwee river system. In the spring, this was an excellent spot for lake trout gathering at the mouth of the river in preparation to spawn. Ben spent about one hundred eighty days per season on the water and knew where to find fish.

The boat moved along the wooded shoreline as the fog was lifting across the lake. Preparing lures and downriggers, the fishing party planned to troll a likely spot along the way. Mike Cadwell, a construction worker from the Twin Cities, watched Thompson attach his fishing line to the downrigger.

"Hopefully all we'll catch is fish with that setup," he said.

"The news said the current official confirmed body count was twenty one bodies total. It gives me the creeps just thinking about it."

Conversation about the recent body discoveries was unavoidable while fishing the lake.

Thompson looked up, shaking his head. "This lake and river system has about nine hundred miles of shoreline combined. It is possible those bodies could have been dropped off a long ways away. I just hope this is the end of it. Two weeks ago there were about ten police boats dragging the main lake around town."

He continued to explain the situation.

"Other boat teams drove the entire shoreline looking for anything that washed up on shore. They didn't find any more bodies after the second day of searching. They have been looking for bodies for eight full days now."

"I hope they will discover this was just a drop site for some maniac serial killer. I wish they would find some clues to another portion of the USA or something. It's kind of scary thinking the killer might still be around here."

"Yeah, no shit," replied Mike, looking around. "That guy must be one sick ticket from what the news reported. This place is pretty remote, but there are still a fair number of summer cottages and private year around cabins on the lake. Kind of makes you wonder."

His brother Jim piped in. "Maybe it's a lake monster or something and not a man at all. Maybe it comes out of the fog and grabs you right off the boat."

He paused for a moment and suddenly lunged at his brother in an attempt to scare him. His younger brother jumped back a little at the grab and shook it off with a chuckle.

Thompson threw the last line overboard. "There are all types of people around here. Some are trappers and Indian folk practically living off the land on the state forest and reservation side."

"Others are doctors, lawyers, and other wealthy people with big lake lots and fancy lake homes on the west and south side by town. Most of the land around the south, west and northwest side is private property." Thompson motioned to the shoreline they were trolling.

"The rest, like this shoreline, is either state forest or reservation land. It could be anyone really. Last I heard there were no Loch Ness monster reports on this lake," he said grinning.

"If there was something out here, I would have seen it by now."

The fish locator suddenly beeped on a school of fish about twenty three feet down. Thompson immediately adjusted the automatic downrigger's line counter to twenty feet.

"Looks like a school of walleyes most likely. Get ready because those lures are dragging about one hundred yards back of that GPS reading."

Sure enough, Mike Cadwell's pole popped off the downrigger cable with a fish on. His brother's line snapped off the cable a few seconds later as the rod tip sprang to life, releasing from the heavy cannonball downrigger weight.

"Alright, we have a double hooked," shouted Thompson.

He never tired of this job even after catching thousands of fish over the years. And two fish on at the same time always increased the excitement and customer satisfaction. Thompson killed the motor and locked in the location on his GPS depth finder.

After a brief battle, two nice five pound walleyed pike were landed. "Not a trophy but a good eater for sure," said Mike with a grin. His brother Jim held his fish up for a quick look before putting it in the live well. "Supper tonight, I love fresh walleye," he exclaimed.

As the charter boat moved up the lake they observed a canoe with a man and dog paddling out from shallow Rice Bay to the north. A large German Shepherd dog sat at the bow of the canoe.

Avoiding the canoe, Thompson turned his boat around for another pass through the school of walleye.

"Let's see if we can find them again," he said with a knowing smile. "Maybe I should give you guys a cheap class on reading depth finders and locating fish. Or, maybe you want to buy a fishing video from me."

The brothers looked at each other. "With only one fish apiece so far, maybe we should throw him overboard," chided Mike.

"Let's give him a break until noon. No more fish by then and we might have to use him as an anchor," chuckled Jim. "Or maybe we should just cut him up for bait. I've heard human chum works well on this lake."

With that they all cracked up. "Okay, Okay, I've heard of demanding customers but you guys are ruthless. And after all the fish I have helped put on your tables in the past. Practically fed your families a couple of years ago," laughed Thompson.

He always enjoyed it when his customers were having a good time. He preferred the customers who chided and had fun over the serious meat on the table type anglers.

After all, no matter how good a fisherman he was, the fish still have to be hungry for success. It would probably be one of many jokes about fishing on Tanner's Lake this season.

Morbid jokes seemed to always be good humor when you are not directly involved. Thompson still couldn't forget the scare he had in the ice shack last winter. He sometimes had nightmares seeing that body pop through the spear hole. He wondered if the case would ever be solved.

Back in Jackson, the police were at a standstill for leads. Forensic medicine verified that all victims died from head trauma and every skull recovered had the teeth extracted. They also determined that twenty of the victims were females of Hispanic decent. The twenty first skeletal set belonged to a female Caucasian with a prior broken and pinned leg. The forensic anthropologist said all of the remains were less than one year old. Many of them appeared to be considerably less than that. They believed at least one set of remains was only about one month old according to forensics. Apparently, the murders had been committed recently and were ongoing. Because of the cold water, most of the remains were still partially covered with flesh. Federal authorities were primarily trying to tie the murders to existing cases across the nation.

So far, no missing person leads matched up on DNA tests to concerned family members. A federal database was checked against those who had offered their DNA for comparisons. All of the bodies were photographed and x-ray's were taken for bone breaks or any other potential information that could help identify them. Unfortunately, dental records were of no assistance as the teeth had been removed.

Federal investigator McCabe and Sheriff Campbell were gathering information locally. McCabe sifted through paper work with the phone receiver pinned to his ear, bending his neck. "I want to know the name and address of everyone in Jackson County who registered for an ice house license last year. I would also like an aerial plat map of Tanner's Lake."

McCabe wanted to interview as many people as he could find who were out on the lake a lot last winter. Maybe somebody had seen something unusual. His own personal belief was that if the bodies were dumped in late summer or fall of the prior year, somebody would have seen one of them before the lake froze. Many of the police investigators had different theories. Some surmised that the depth of the lake could have held the bodies down for months until the lake turned over. Tanner's Lake was sixty feet deep in some spots. Lake turn over was Mother Nature's way of providing life giving oxygen to the water and helping the fish population thrive.

During fall turnover, when the lake reaches approximately thirty nine degrees on the surface, the heavier water begins to sink, displacing the warmer water below it. When the displaced water from the bottom of the lake is on the surface, it continues to cool as the temperature drops and winter approaches. Eventually the lake is a uniform temperature in the mid thirties and the surface water freezes, capping the lake in an insulation of ice. This process mixes fresh oxygen from decaying matter off the lake bottom into the entire lake mass. The water mixing process replenishes the deep water with life giving nutrients allowing fish to return to the depths where they will spend the winter months. In the spring when the ice melts on the surface a spring turnover occurs. The colder melting ice water on top sinks causing the lake to flip again. This process could hold a body down deep for a long time or push it to the surface when the ice melted.

It appears that Tanner's Lake residents witnessed what spring turnover could do to a submerged body first hand. It was a big lake and the bodies could have been dumped anytime in the last year. It was also possible they could go undetected in a body of water this size. His gut feeling still made him think someone would have found at least one body during the height of the boating season. But maybe not in early November, as very few boats are seen on the lake as the temperature begins to drop. Minnesota sportsmen are busy pursing other actives when fall arrives. Many put away the fishing rods and uncase their hunting weapons that time of year.

McCabe paused for a moment as the young lady on the other end of the phone wrote down the information he requested.

"Also, any resident information I can get from the tax rolls. I want to know who lives or owns property on the lake. Sometime tomorrow would be great if you can gather that up by then."

"That should be no problem Agent McCabe. We will have it ready for you tomorrow by noon."

"I really appreciate your help. Thanks."

McCabe hung up the phone and walked into Sheriff Campbell's office. "The County departments are going to supply us with information on who owns the private property around the lake and where it is located. I am also going to find out who purchased ice house registrations last year."

The Sheriff shook his head.

"I still think this was just a place to get rid of the bodies for some nut. I know most of the people around here, and I just can't see anyone doing something like this."

McCabe, a trained serial murder investigator, responded.

"No one ever wants to think there is evil lurking in the backyard. That is human nature. I just want to ask some questions and hang around the area for awhile. I plan on renting a few cabins around the lake and getting some fishing in as well."

McCabe picked his notebook up from the desk and continued.

"Maybe something will jump out at me. Besides, if this individual has left the area, there are a lot of investigators working this case waiting for him to make a mistake. I'll keep you posted as to my whereabouts, but I don't want your deputies coming out to visit me. I want to remain as anonymous and under cover as possible. You know what I mean, just some good old boy out on vacation trying to relax and catch a few fish. Okay?"

Sheriff Campbell appeared somewhat annoyed, "I guess, but if I hear about any type of harassment from people on the lake, I will make a visit personally. People come up here to get away from crime in the big cities and have a good time. They don't need to be worrying about a serial killer who is probably not even around here anymore. You know what I mean, some street clothes cop giving them the third degree interrogation about stuff they know nothing about."

McCabe grabbed his coat and walked out of the office. "No problem Sheriff. That is not my style anyway. I'll be in touch."

The sky looked like rain as he hopped into an unmarked four by four Ford F150. The truck had a locked hard top covering the box. He first drove to the town beach where three bodies had been found.

Gazing along the shoreline he viewed the nice lake homes along the beach and lining the southern most bay. Most of the bodies had turned up on or near this end of the lake, he thought.

So far, most of the investigation had been centered in this area. Sheriff Campbell had questioned many neighboring residents of the beach, to see if they had observed anything unusual.

The wind blew a steady chop of white caps from the north as he looked up the narrow lake to the disappearing horizon. The lake map on the truck seat showed the north side of the lake. It appeared to be about thirty miles by water. Flanagan's Resort was the northern most resort listed on the map. Just off the Big Stone Indian Reservation and state forest to the north and east.

McCabe started his car and headed over to the courthouse to pick up his paperwork. Across the street from the courthouse was a small outfitters store. He decided to go there first and give them a little more time running his reports.

A store clerk approached him, "Can I help you?"

"I'm interested in a fishing pole and some tackle."

The clerk led him over to the poles and tackle. "Did you have anything special in mind?"

He picked up a fishing lure for a closer look. "I need a rod and reel, tackle box, some lures and a landing net." McCabe tried on a fishing hat as the clerk suggested some rods and reels.

"I'll take this one," he said, whipping the pole back and forth.

After filling a tackle box with assorted lures, he placed the box on the counter with a baseball style fishing cap and a rain poncho.

The clerk pointed out the landing nets and he added a medium net to the mix as well. As he rang up the assorted items, McCabe inquired about cabin resort rentals.

"Are you looking for a big resort or a smaller private cabin?"

"There are plenty of both usually available."

McCabe took his eyes off the large stuffed black bear in the corner of the room. "I guess just a small cabin where I can rent a fishing boat."

The clerk pulled out a paper tourist map from under the counter and circled a few suggestions for him.

"Go ahead and keep the map."

McCabe looked at the map and Flanagan's Resort was not circled.

"What do you think of this little place on the north side of the lake?"

"I will be leaving for home from that side of the lake anyway."

The clerk shook his head. "Don't normally recommend Flanagan's Resort unless you're a local. Lots of backwoods good old boys in the joint."

"There has been an occasional conflict of interest with the neighboring Indian folk who also go there. Usually over the fishing and netting laws allowed on the reservation. Some of the non-Indian folk think it impacts the lakes fishing as it is pretty liberal with gill netting allowed and some high limits."

He bagged McCabe's purchase and went on. "The Indian's are allowed so many thousand pounds of fish a year. Once that limit is met, the State Department of Natural Resources stops the take. A lot of the non reservation people get mad as they have to throw back half of their fish in the protected slot limits. Mix in a few beers on a hot day in late summer when the fishing is slow and a night at the bar in a mixed crowd. It's a recipe for a fight, usually started by a drunk who got skunked fishing that day because there are no fish left in the lake. The reservation borders Flanagan's land and he gets customers from both sides. These fishing arguments go back a long way. I don't envy that Flanagan fellow and what he has to put up with to stay in business."

The clerk paused for a moment, "Nothing to concern yourself about anyway. The fishing is just as good on the west side of the lake near this rocky reef."

He circled the reef on the map. "I just think you might have a better time around this area. If you don't understand the ways of some of these local people, you might be looking for trouble. They don't think like your average tourist on that north side."

"Is that right," responded McCabe. "Thank you for the tip, I guess there is plenty of lake to fish. More than I can do in a couple of weeks, that's for sure."

McCabe grabbed his gear and headed out the door. He opened the truck cab and threw the gear behind the seat next to an uncased short barreled shotgun mounted on brackets.

"Flanagan's bar eh? Sounds like my kind of place," he said to himself. After completing one more quick stop to retrieve his requested paperwork he began driving north.

The forty mile road along the west side of the lake to Flanagan's Resort wound through the private cabin and large resort district first. The final twenty miles were more remote.

Once in awhile he would pass a private driveway down to the lake from a cabin. Eventually he came to a gravel road with a small faded wood sign nailed to a tree. The red painted sign read Flanagan's – three miles, with an arrow pointing to the right.

As he entered the resort, an old dilapidated sign hung over the entrance. It read "Flanagan's Resort" in faded green letters with shamrock notations on each side of the sign. Approximately ten small log cabins with stone fireplaces lined the road into the resort main log lodge. The lake looked bright blue through the trees as he passed along the cabins.

The main lodge had a totem pole sign with one arrow pointing "Office" to the right. A second sign simply said "Bar" with an arrow across the deck pointed to the left. Another said "Docks" and pointed to the lake. The bottom arrow said "Cabins" and pointed up the road he had just come down.

McCabe parked his car and walked into the small office. Through another door, a woman approximately fifty years of age entered the room. "Hello, I was wondering if you had any cabins vacant?" asked McCabe.

"We have five rooms left to choose from," she replied. "The place is empty this year with all the bad news."

She pulled out a paper lodge map and circled the available rooms. "Which do you like best?" asked McCabe.

She smiled and said, "number seven, but not for any reasons you would like it. It just has some old memories. I would say you would prefer number ten, way on the end. It is the most secluded. They are all identical cabins and come with a sixteen foot fishing boat and a twenty five horse powered outboard motor."

McCabe raised his cap up a notch while thinking.

"How about number two here close to the resort docks and bar?

"I don't want to be too far from everything."

He thought he had a better chance mingling with the locals if he was near the bar and docks. She looked him in the eye, "Number two it is," and handed him a key off the wall.

She explained the rental rates and other amenities of the resort.

"The tavern is just around the corner, if you get too much peace and quiet. There is a ten dollar per day dock charge for the boat but the first six gallons of gas are free. After that you can fill up at our dock pump if you need it. The cabin is eighty dollars a night with a two night minimum this time of year. I will need a credit card or cash in advance."

McCabe completed the required check-in paperwork and put the charges on his personal credit card.

"My husband Dan is usually working the tavern or the docks when he is not repairing things in the cabins. You will see him behind the bar usually. He can get you beer, bait, and gas. The big three top money makers around this joint everyone seems to need."

She held out her hand and introduced herself. "By the way, my name is Mary Flanagan. I can provide whatever you might need in the cabin for linens. I also cook breakfast and dinner at the restaurant every day for guests on the meal plan."

McCabe responded, "The name is Jack McCabe, another fellow Irishman just seeking some peace and quiet in the great north woods. Thank you, Mrs. Flanagan, for the fine service you are providing. You have a grand resort here indeed. I bet you are a great cook too."

She smiled and watched him walk out the door across to the cabins. She couldn't help but wonder how a polite gentleman of his nature would do in a dump like this. She could already tell he could sling the malarkey with the best of them.

Inside, the room was clean and simple, nothing but a log framed double bed and a small kitchen area with a couple of chairs next to the stone fireplace. Outside was a dirt path to a small dock with a boat and motor tied to it. Just outside the cabin door was a small cedar deck with a barbecue and two chairs tucked neatly in the corner.

This place is perfect, he thought to himself. It would be a nice cabin for a romantic evening sometime on a vacation date. After unloading his groceries, McCabe cracked a beer and started a fire.

He had grown up as a boy in the rural Minnesota lake country. He sometimes wondered how he wound up with a job chasing insane criminals in large metropolitan areas around the country. This would be a fun change, investigating a case like this one. Just being near the water made him feel good and brought back fond memories of time spent on the water as a kid. Sometimes his life in the big city made him wish he was still living in a rural area. The hustle and bustle of the rat race was completely left behind in a setting like this.

As the sun went down on Tanner's Lake, he studied the topographical map intently while thinking to himself. If the killer is in the area, the crime will happen again. This type of serial killer never quits until they are caught. They might stop for awhile, but they never quit.

If I am going to have a chance at this nut, I will have to make myself a potential victim. An attractive easy target, someone too stupid to realize the danger until it's too late. I need to almost become bait, for whoever this killer might be. As serial investigations of this nature progressed, the serial profile usually developed as well. His experience told him the murders would continue and a profile would emerge. Often times the serial killer would contact the press with information. That had not happened yet in this case. He believed that this killer was in the area and not using the lake as a dump zone for bodies. The victims had also been killed at different times through the winter. This told him that it was not a mass dump of bodies all killed at the same time. This killer was methodically operating and McCabe's experience told him that would continue.

Opening his brief case, he laid out the forensic reports on the kitchen table and reviewed them. Comparing the police dragging reports against the forensic reports, he focused on the potential time of death and where the bodies were found. Hanging a large Tanner's Lake map he purchased at the tackle shop, he made notes with a red pen. First he circled all the locations where the bodies were discovered. They were scattered from the south end of the lake to the north, with the majority near the south side town beach. He went through the forensic report and wrote down the probable date of death inside each circled location.

As he completed this exercise, he noticed a pattern developing. It seemed the oldest bodies appeared to be closer to the south end of the lake. Most of them were found near the town beach of Jackson. The bodies that were less than three months old were more in the central portion of the lake. The most recent victims were not far from his current location on the north end of the lake. He was not sure what this meant, but there were a couple of possibilities that immediately came to mind.

Maybe the killer was getting rid of the bodies in random locations on the lake. Possibly some of the older victims had been dumped by boat off the south end. Or, maybe the bodies were drifting on their own with lake currents and a steady breeze usually from the north. If the latter theory was true, that would put the killer more than likely operating on the northern half of the lake. If that was the case, Flanagan's Resort would be a good place to start investigating.

Taking a long draw on his beer, he put his feet up on the table to relax. He wondered if his current occupation was an unhealthy one. After all, it was extremely dangerous opening yourself up to a deranged psychopathic killer. He was almost killed on a case six years ago and was stabbed in the shoulder. It was a case in Milwaukee where FBI agents had tracked a guy that was killing homeless people and dumping them in railroad yards. He eventually tracked the suspect to a sleazy apartment in downtown

Milwaukee. When he went into the man's home to question him, all was going pretty well at first. Until he noticed a railroad spike on the man's desk being used as a paper weight. When he inquired about it, the man seemed tense and suddenly without warning lunged at him with a knife, slashing him in the shoulder before he could get his weapon drawn. The blade had come close to his throat as he reacted to get out of harm's way. He managed to take the suspect alive, shooting him once in each leg before arresting him. He needed him alive to prove he was the killer. The man eventually confessed to eighteen murders and was serving life without parole in the federal penitentiary. McCabe had received eighty-two stitches in his shoulder wound and had lost quite a bit of blood by the time reinforcements had arrived. Not nearly as much blood as his arrested suspect, as he made sure he was not going anywhere. Sometimes being a federal agent was a risky business, no doubt about it. Getting people like this off the street was the bottom line on his job. He couldn't worry about the risk.

There was great gratification in knowing the criminal was stopped and lives were saved. It was always worth it whatever the risk involved when a case finally ended. That guy would have continued to kill until he was arrested. Interrogation after his arrest showed his serial killer behavior pattern and he was a classic example. He really had nothing against the homeless. They were just easy targets for him to abduct and kill, supplying his consuming need for power. This man knew right from wrong, as psychopaths do. He just did not care and lacked any conscience or remorse for his actions. Frankly stated, the psychopath enjoyed killing.

A pure psychotic, serial killer, was the other possible type of profile he might be dealing with. Psychotic individuals were a minority among serial killers, and the individual would be considered legally insane. Of all the serial murder cases McCabe had investigated, none had matched the psychotic profile. Psychopathic serial killers tended to blend into society and were difficult to identify as killers until you got very close to them.

By definition, most serial killers are male Caucasians in their twenties or thirties. They tend to kill one or two people at a time and usually someone who is vulnerable. Normally they kill three or more victims who are complete strangers and they do it slowly over an extended period of time. Some serial killers have an obsession with law enforcement or authoritative figures. Often times, they make contact with the police to gain attention. In this case, there had been no police or media contact whatsoever. McCabe did not have much to go on at this point. He wondered what profile the Tanner's Lake killer would have.

A psychotic killer might be easier to identify in society, but they would be no less dangerous. He did not find much comfort in realizing that it might be obvious the person was crazy when confronting them. The removal of the teeth made him wonder if this would be his first truly psychotic serial killer case. A truly insane person was scary, as they could be capable of anything. Once insanity takes over, they can be the most ruthless killers on the planet. History books had told him of horrible cannibal killers that fill into this profile. It was questionable whether some of them could even be classified as human from their heinous acts of violence. In some ways, McCabe was glad they were by far the minority profile in serial murder investigations.

He removed the shoulder holster holding the nine millimeter automatic pistol and laid it on the small bedside table. He crawled under the covers and listened to the loons singing on the lake. Before long he was drifting off to sleep wondering what tomorrow would bring. He planned on making some contacts and exploring the lake.

3

Morning broke with the call of loons singing on the lake. McCabe clamored out of bed and looked out the window at the sun rising over the trees across the lake. A beautiful day to explore the lake and try a little fishing he thought. After a quick breakfast he walked down to his boat and threw in his newly purchased fishing tackle.

The motor started on the third pull as he adjusted the tiller outboard. He motored slowly out from the dock in reverse and turned the boat around to face the big lake. Shifting to the forward gear, he turned the throttle handle all the way down and sped out on the big lake.

The sixteen foot deep v-hull boat moved quickly through the calm morning water. He had heard about twenty five miles per hour was a good estimate for a lightly loaded boat of this size, pushed by a twenty five horse power motor.

The boat was fast enough to get him off the lake in a reasonable amount of time if a big storm started to crop up. That was all he cared about. Rain was one thing to get caught in while out on a big lake, but lightning was downright scary, and something he would rather avoid all together.

The boat motored towards Rice Bay on the reservation side of the lake. He studied the lake map and his current location as the boat moved into the bay. When he entered the calm water on the leeward east side of the bay, he could see it was only about 5 feet deep. He killed the motor and glided toward a patch of lily pads about thirty feet from shore.

As the boat slowed he made a cast to the shoreline with an artificial minnow. After several tries he changed bait. He continued to throw a variety of crank baits about ten feet off shore and slowly retrieve them. For some odd reason, he felt uneasy as the boat drifted along the thick woods lining the shore. He was the only boat for as far as the eye could see. He almost felt like he was the first man to ever fish this bay.

The glowing yellow eyes tracked the boat as it drifted twenty feet off shore. Tiny sunfish chased his spinner bait through the clear water nipping at hooks as he retrieved the cast. McCabe amused himself by dragging the bait around the boat, watching the little fish.

The boat drifted near a dead tree extending out over the water about ten feet. Looking like a good spot, he dropped the anchor and changed to a floating surface lure. His cast was perfect, dropping the popper right under the overhanging tree.

This time the bait change paid off. The shaded water beneath the tree exploded seconds after the lure landed. It looked to be a nice smallmouth bass breaking the water's surface in a violent attack. Commonly called "Smallies" by the locals, and known for their ability to fight. The fish headed for deeper water taking out line on the ultra light spinning rig. Standing up in the boat, McCabe set the hook and began to battle the running fish.

The yellow eyes in the trees began to move closer as McCabe fought the fish. Leaning over the boat he brought the fish up to the boat. With line and pole taught in his left hand, he reached down and grabbed the tired fish by the mouth with his free hand.

Admiring his catch, it looked to be about a six pound small mouth. A nice fish in anyone's book, considering the current Minnesota state record for small mouth bass was eight pounds.

Just as he was about to release the fish, he was suddenly struck from behind. A sharp cutting pain to the back of his head knocked him to the boat floor. The fish flopped in the boat as he went down.

Momentarily dazed, he got up on one knee and looked around. A bald eagle stared down at him ominously perched atop a dead tree thirty feet away. The figure in the shadows moved closer behind the trees to the left of the boat.

McCabe was unaware of the figure and focused his attention on the bird. Blood oozed from a large gash in the back lower part of his neck. Scrambling to the front of the boat he frantically pulled up the anchor rope.

The bald eagle swooped in again as the human prey turned its back to the bird. This time, he heard the wings and saw the bird come in from the corner of his eye. Instinctively, he raised his forearm up over his head. The bird's sharp talons ripped his shirt with the arm block.

McCabe grabbed a canoe paddle swinging it as the large bird sailed away. "Come on you son-of-a-bitch. Let's play some bird ball." He pressed his bleeding right forearm to his thigh watching the bird's movement.

The eagle circled high overhead as he finished pulling in the anchor. Turning to the rear of the boat, another lightning fast strike grazed his face cutting his forehead. It was a different bird on this attack. Whirling around, he grabbed his pistol and fired as the rising thunderbolt rose into the sky like a jet fighter plane. In the sky it looked much smaller than the eagle.

McCabe pulled desperately on the outboard motor starting rope. The engine sputtered on each pull. This time the two birds attacked at the same time. The smaller bird flashed by his face cutting his left eyebrow as his hand went up too late. The eagle hit him a split second later up around his neck and shoulders almost knocking him overboard. He pulled his gun once more and fired a single futile shot as both birds rocketed out of site.

Yanking frantically on the outboard rope, blood ran down his face and into his eyes. His head rotated rapidly scanning the sky as if on a swivel. Pointing his revolver at the two birds now circling high above him, he fired two more rounds.

Suddenly, a shrill high pitched scream echoed from the shady wooded shoreline. McCabe reactively hit the boat floor in terror. Obviously shaken by this encounter, he peeked over the boat side wall, keeping low with gun drawn.

Behind the rocky wooded shoreline he could hear something big walking parallel to him in the brush. The boat was drifting closer to shore. Minutes seemed like hours as he waited with gun ready, but nothing materialized. As he drifted even closer, the shoreline became totally silent again. He was only about ten feet out with the boat almost beached. He sensed something was there but could see only trees.

After a few minutes, he reached over with his free hand and pulled out the choke on the motor. Another yank on the cord and the motor popped and roared. He throttled the motor back and shifted to reverse, churning backwards out of the lily pads.

The boat moved slowly away from shore as McCabe remained on the boat floor with gun drawn. He reached up from the floor operating the tiller as he watched the shoreline move farther away.

At about thirty yards out, he sat up and turned the boat around. The birds were nowhere in sight. McCabe's head rapidly glanced from the sky back to the shoreline. He hit the throttle and the boat sped across the lake back towards Flanagan's Resort.

Blood streamed down his head, face and arm as he crossed the big lake. He cursed the birds as he wiped the blood from his eyes with a piece of torn shirt. As McCabe pulled into the sheltered bay at Flanagan's docks, Ben Thompson's charter boat was also moving into the harbor. They met at the resort docks as agent McCabe beached his boat and stumbled out on shore still bleeding profusely. Thompson immediately assisted him, throwing a spare towel from his boat to the bleeding man. "What happened to you?" he asked.

McCabe held the towel over his wounded forearm. The cuts on his forehead and eyebrow had stopped bleeding from holding his ripped shirt on the wounds. "Maybe you can tell me," said McCabe. "I've never been attacked by birds before. They just started diving at my head. It looked like some kind of hawk and a bald eagle. It scared the shit out of me. I hate little birds when they do that around a nest. This was totally nuts."

Obviously still excited, McCabe continued to ramble on. "It was unbelievable when they dove at me. These birds were actually trying to take my head off. I blocked the big one with my forearm and it clawed the shit out of me."

He paused for a second, "I could barely see them they were so fast. I mean incredibly fast. What the hell is going on around here? Don't those damn things have any food or what?"

Thompson grabbed the first aid kit off his boat. "Let's go inside and have a look at your arm. You got a room here?" McCabe grabbed the keys from his pocket and pointed towards his cabin.

Inside, Thompson looked over his wounds. "Your forehead, eyebrow and neck appear to be just a deep scratch. Your forearm cut is quite deep as you can see. Do you want to go to town and see if you need stitches?"

McCabe took a good look at the gash on his forearm. "I have had worse, let's just tape them up with a gauze bandage if you don't mind. It should be okay. I don't want to waste my vacation at the doctor's office. I really appreciate the help. I didn't pack any first aid stuff. By the way, my name is Jack McCabe." He held his hand out. Thompson cut the gauze wrap and shook his hand.

"Ben Thompson, I own a guide service on the south end of the lake." He quickly finished wrapping and taping the bandage over the wound.

"Let me buy you a beer for all the trouble," said McCabe. "No trouble, but I will take a beer if you will tell me more about what exactly happened. Sounds like you have quite a story to tell," replied Thompson.

As they walked into Flanagan's tavern, a couple of old timers were perched at the smoky bar. A pool table graced the bar floor with a row of booths on the far wall. The bar looked like the original woodwork from the golden area of taverns in the 1930s and '40s.

McCabe and Thompson pulled up a couple of stools at the bar next to an Indian fellow. Flanagan recognized Thompson. "How is it going Ben? Getting any fish this year?"

Thompson looked up. "Hi Dan, the fishing is great. I just can't find enough customers to take out this year. I took a couple of regulars out on the opener and we caught quite a few. They're renting a boat now and have been hammering them all week. They're getting them up around Rice Bay. Not too far from here."

McCabe piped into the conversation.

"I'll take a genuine draft and whatever he is drinking."

Ben acknowledged, "I'll have the same. Thanks."

Flanagan got the beers for the men and made change from a twenty. McCabe left the money on the bar for the next round.

Thompson turned to McCabe. "So birds attacked you on the lake today?"

McCabe sipped his beer. "That's right. I had just caught a really nice smallmouth in Rice Bay. Then all of a sudden out of nowhere, wham! Something smacks me in the back of the neck."

He swiveled his head, "Still hurts a little bit. The next thing I know I'm looking up at this bird in a tree from the floor of the boat." The group listened in amazement.

"It was a bald eagle, a big beautiful bird. At first, I wasn't even sure if that's what hit me, but I heard wings and saw it flying back to the tree as I was getting up. Then I turned my back and the thing swooped in at me again. This time I saw it and got my arm up. That's where it nailed me in the forearm."

"Wow. That is incredible," said Thompson. Flanagan and Thompson both looked at each other with eyes wide.

"Then as I started pulling up the anchor another bird buzzed me. They both came at me one more time as I was starting the motor."

McCabe went on with his story. "I heard some weird animal scream on shore too during all this. Finally, I got the motor started and headed back here nursing my wounds. No sign of the birds anywhere by then."

"They were probably going for your catch. That is really, really unusual though. I've heard of owls and hawks hitting fur hats on people's heads in the winter woods before," commented Flanagan.

"You know, like those rabbit skin bomber hats the dog musher's often wear. I guess it can look like food to a confused or stupid bird."

The Native American man, listening intently, looked at the group of men. "I have heard of such a thing before," he said. McCabe looked at the middle aged man. "Okay, can you tell me about it?"

George White Owl began telling a long drawn out story to the group. "About sixty years ago, in 1949, there was a dispute between the Indians and the local settlers over the fishing rights on the lake. Because of prejudice on both sides, the dispute became violent. From the white man's perspective, gill netting was commercial fishing and hurting the sport fishing and resort business. The Native Americans contested that this was their god given right and that their forefathers had been gill netting fish with hand-made nets before white men ever discovered Tanner's Lake."

McCabe interjected. "So what does that mean?"

"It means White Owl is going to tell one of his old Indian stories," chuckled Flanagan.

The Indian man continued on. "The white resort owners and fishermen held protests on the south border of the reservation which extends out one mile into Rice Bay. Non-Indians are not allowed to fish there and they still aren't today, but it is never enforced so people still do.

Anyway, the protesters crossed the one mile water boundary one night on the reservation land and beached their boats in Rice Bay. The bay was a primary netting area for the tribal people. They cut the Indian gill nets in the bay on their way to shore."

Mr. White Owl paused recalling how the story went down.

"Then they went looking for some people to beat up and put a good scare into them. Well, they got more than they bargained for as they ran into a band of seven young Indian men living on the reservation. A full blown fight broke out with about a dozen people on each side eventually going at it. Several people were badly injured in the melee and one white man died from striking his head on a rock during the fight. White retaliation followed a week later."

McCabe listened intently. "So what happened?"

"Initially, three Native American tribal leaders were dragged off the reservation and lynched not far from here. The mob leaders claimed the men were responsible for the death of their friend. A tribal group trying to stop the lynching arrived minutes too late. When they saw what had been done, gun fire erupted. When it was over, four more white men were dead and two more Indians."

Flanagan refilled White Owls tap beer as he continued.

"Government authorities intervened the next day, ruling that the Indians had a signed one hundred year old treaty that allowed gill netting. It was part of a deal the government agreed to for making the Indian people live on the reservation. After that, anyone caught harassing the Indians about fishing was arrested and dealt with harshly."

McCabe looked at him, thinking he was a bit confused and rambling on with his story. "So what does this have to do with birds attacking me?"

"Stiff penalties were imposed and this put an end to the dispute. This also started the Indian legend of Chief Grey Wolf, father of one of the lynched victims. It was his only son of seven children and he was crushed. In his despair over the loss of his only son, he put a curse on any white men who cross the reservation boundary leading into Rice Bay. The curse stated that any white man venturing into reservation waters without permission would be eventually devoured by the creatures of the forest."

George White Owl looked at a lake map where McCabe was fishing.

"You were across the reservation boundary in Rice Bay. You should not go back to this place."

Flanagan wiped the bar surface and chuckled.

"I must say old George here sure knows a lot of shit. But then again, maybe those birds just wanted your fish in the bottom of the boat."

He gave the men a couple more beers and went on. "My grandfather owned this resort in 1949. He was right in the middle of the whole thing and tried to stop the mob. They staged the attack right here at this very tavern. It is a true story."

Dan Flanagan wiped the counter and continued.

"They beat him up before they left because they thought he was going to call the cops. It put him in the hospital for two weeks. They were definitely a bunch of assholes. But my grandfather never mentioned or heard of any curse bullshit."

The men sipped their beers and traded stories of big fish and lake lore passed down over the years. Soon Thompson downed his final beer.

"I've got to head home gentlemen. Tomorrow is another day on the water."

He wished McCabe good luck fishing and jokingly told him to watch out for Purple Martins, a small bird found around the lake country resorts. It was well known for swooping and diving around people while feeding on mosquitoes.

With a laughing exit, Thompson made his way down to his boat and headed for home.

McCabe turned to George White Owl and asked him more about the legend.

"If you want, tomorrow you can visit the reservation with me. You can talk to my grandfather who knew Chief Grey Wolf. He is a very wise man who knows much about these things. If you want to come along, meet me in the tavern at noon tomorrow. You buy me more beer tonight, and I will take you there tomorrow. Maybe you can buy me lunch tomorrow too."

McCabe went along with his con game and accepted the invitation. Probably just a regular Flanagan's bar patron working him for beers, but it was a way to get on the reservation inconspicuously.

He would get to know the people who lived around here, which was what he originally set out to do. It would not amaze him if the killer turned out to be someone off the reservation. Those people kind of existed in their own little world without many people knowing what goes on inside their boundary. At this point he certainly had nothing better to go on.

McCabe swallowed the last of his beer and thanked White Owl. "I would be honored to learn more about your people." McCabe suddenly stopped for a minute and turned toward the middle aged sun wrinkled Indian man, "I thought you said I should never go to Rice Bay again." George smiled at the three beers McCabe had lined up for him.

"This is very true. You must not ever go into the bay again without Native American tribal permission. That is the key to the curse. Remember, I am inviting you to the reservation. I am an Indian and a member of the tribe."

McCabe nodded at him and walked out the tavern door muttering under his breath as he looked at his wallet.

"Right, I think I get it. You are a wise tribal elder who works for beer. I hope it is worth spending my time."

The lake air felt cool on his skin as he walked down to the cabin and turned in for the night. He looked across the lake at Rice Bay from his doorstep. Not a single light illuminated the far shoreline. It was pitch black with nothing but the sound of waves slashing the rocks on shore.

He wondered what it must have been like the night in 1949 when the mob attacked. He thought about the Indian legend as he crawled into his bed and closed his eyes. A distant pack of timber wolves howled in the night as he drifted off to sleep.

4

Breathing heavily, the large man hustled up the wooded hillside knocking brush and branches from his face. Trotting behind him, a large wolf dog hybrid followed him up the hill. Climbing the steep hill to the crest, a large black crow acknowledged his presence. Caw… Caw… Caw… announced the bird in rapid succession.

Five raptures waited at the mouth of the cave as the huge bearded man approached. His clothes were ragged buckskin and his hair was a wild shoulder length entanglement. The birds sat perched on tree branches in front of the limestone cave. The foliage of the trees obscured the cave entrance from above and below.

A small rock ledge along a fifty foot high limestone cliff led to the cave entrance. It was no more than three feet wide. The ledge was concealed by a thick growth of sumac plants growing from the cliff's side. On top of the cliff, more sumac trees tangled with vines obscured the cliff completely from view. To the unwary, a sheer drop would mean certain death to the rocks and trees below.

The man crawled under the sumac on the top of the cliff to a three foot wide rock ledge. Once on the ledge, the sumac had been trimmed to form a sort of tunnel-like trail. The big man's eyes were dark and piercing as he limped along the path.

Pointing at the wolf dog he spoke in a low gruff voice, "guard the cliff." The massive animal trotted up to the outside of the ledge opening and laid down eyeing the hill.

The big man stopped and stuck his arm into a large crevice in the rock cliff. He groaned as he threw his three hundred pound frame against a large slate rock about six inches thick along the ledge. The large rock moved with apparent ease, sliding parallel to the ledge on cut grooves in the cave floor.

Once moved, it revealed the entrance to a small cave. He stooped down and walked through the large opening. Inside, the cave walls were illuminated by sunlight from the open entrance. In the middle of the room, a flat piece of rock slate lay across two bigger rocks.

He threw down a bundle of traps from his buckskin pack and walked back out of the cave with the pet hawk perched on his arm. He spoke to the hawk as he walked down the path.

"Maybe I should let you peck out their eyes. Would you like that my little bird?"

He began walking down the trail and called the wolf dog back to his side. The big animal trotted up and followed behind him. "It is time for your lunch."

At the base of the cliff a larger opening was cleared of the thick vegetation. It made a room-like area with walls and ceiling consisting of vines and wild raspberry bushes. They were so thick you could not see through them.

Two men were bound and naked, staked to the ground in the open area. Three hawks stood tethered at attention on stumps watching the men knowingly. The big hovering man gazed down at one of the staked men and kicked him in the ribs.

"How would you like to die my friend? In my world, trespassing is punishable by death. Possibly my dog can explain my point better."

He pointed at the bound man's leg and called his big wolf dog.

"Lobo, left leg meat," he said in command like tone. The wolf instantly sprang on his command, ripping the man's left foot apart.

The staked and gagged victim attempted a muffled screamed in agonizing pain as the wolf dog bit through his ankle crunching the bone. His head shook back and forth as he was being devoured alive.

In seconds, the wolf tore the foot completely off and trotted to the side of the room with his prize. He laid down, gnawing on the foot like a tame dog with a bone. The second man watched in horror as blood spurted from the severed limb. The injured victim wiggled in pain.

The huge man roared in laughter at the pain his victim was experiencing. "You are a lucky man my friend because your death will be relatively quick. Your friend staked here next to you will not be so lucky. It could take all week for him to meet his maker. You are really very fortunate."

With that the mad man threw his head back in an uproarious sick guttural laughter. His long filthy hair flew back from his face revealing the dark eyes of a psychotic lunatic.

He spit on the bleeding man and pulled a small silver bell from his buckskin clothing. Approaching each hawk, he released the leather tethering from their talons, allowing them freedom to fly. Then he rang the silver bell.

"Dinner time my feathered friends."

The three hawks jumped from their perches in a frantic pecking brawl at the man's naked body. In seconds his flesh was ripped open from limb to limb by the formidable talons and sharp beaks designed for tearing flesh. The man lost consciousness nearly immediately from loss of blood.

The mad man looked at his next victim in wonderment with a quizzical look on his face.

"The birds and scavengers will pick your friend to a complete skeleton in a few days. The fun part about it is you can watch it all happen with a front row seat!"

"When the maggots begin their work, maybe I will even give you a taste." He grabbed his remaining victim and sat him upright tied to a tree with both legs spread apart and staked to the ground.

Tied at the ankles and thighs, he could barely move. The big grey wolf dog continued to gnaw at the dead man's foot as if it were a domestic dog with a steak bone now stripped of meat.

The birds were ripping large pieces of flesh from the dead man's body and gobbling it down frantically as if in competition with the others to get their share before it was gone.

"We must leave you alone now to enjoy dinner with your dead companion. But first I must introduce you to my smallest friends."

His victim was helpless, bound and gagged with his clothing completely stripped. The mad man pulled a glass jar from his burlap sack on the ground and opened it. Tipping the jar he lightly tapped the bottom over his prisoner's chest. A pile of crawling insects spilled across the man's torso.

"Wood ticks will be your personal guests while we are gone.

I do expect you to be a good host and treat them right. Remember, any friend of mine is a friend of yours!"

Tears ran down the bound man's face as hundreds of wood ticks began to disperse and crawl over his entire body.

The crazy man's laugh boomed across the forest as he emptied the rest of the jar on him. With eyes bulging outward in fear, the victim squirmed and then closed his eyes. As the demented man was leaving he turned to look at his victim.

"By the way, my name is Prometheus the Griffin, master of the forest and enforcer of the Indian land. Jack of all trades you might say, trapper, fisherman, hawker, scholar and today executioner!

You, my friend, should read your fishing regulations closer. It is illegal to fish on Indian waters. I am pleased to make your acquaintance young man. Remember, if I can be of any assistance just holler!"

He laughed at his own banter.

"Oh! I forgot. You can't holler, can you?" he said sarcastically.

"Well, I will be back in about a week to see how you are treating my small guests. I hope you feed them well while I am gone. Maybe we can all have dinner together when I return. Unless they are so full they are ready to burst."

He held up the little silver bell and tinkled it. "Remember, don't be late for supper."

The obsessed man lumbered up the trail out of sight, laughing at his own twisted amusement. He entered the cave and picked up his fishing pole. Next to the pole laid a rifle and a bag of steel animal traps spilled half open.

Removing his buckskin poncho he changed into a nylon blue jacket. Pushing the round slate rock over the cave opening, he started up the cliff. Fishing pole in hand, he emerged from the cliff ledge with his wolf dog following behind him.

He walked downhill through the woods about five hundred yards to the lake below. His canoe was hidden next to a small rowboat pulled up on shore about fifteen feet.

He uncovered the pine boughs from the canoe and pushed it in the water. His wolf dog jumped in and lay down in the front of the canoe. He proceeded to paddle east toward a public landing on the state forest side of the lake.

Using the canoeing J-stroke, he maneuvered the boat on a straight line, expertly cutting through the dead calm water. After a thirty minute paddle the landing was now in sight. Once at the boat ramp, the big man beached his canoe and walked up to his parked truck.

He threw his fishing pole in the back and drove the truck down to the waters edge. Another car pulled in with a boat and trailer attached. "How is the fishing?" said a young man in his thirties.

The Griffin smiled and answered. "I am just out for a paddle. But they are biting in Rice Bay I have heard."

With that the big strong man lifted his canoe to the wooden crossbars on his pickup and slid the boat up with ease. He eyed the young man for his reaction.

"Unfortunately, that is in reservation water, I am pretty sure," the young fisherman replied. "Not supposed to go in there."

The big man smiled at him. "Maybe you are right my wise friend. In the spring fishing is usually good across the lake too."

Prometheus climbed in his truck and started the motor. "Good luck fishing." The truck left the state forest and bounced down an old stub logging road to a dead end about three miles into the woods.

After a one mile hike south through the woods, he arrived at a small log cabin hunting shack. Inside, it was dirty with a bunk in one corner and a kitchen cluttered with old dirty dishes. In the corner stood a wood stove with a stove pipe going up through the roof. Large steel animal traps hung from the walls. A mouse scurried across the floor as he entered.

He laid his big frame on the lower bunk bed and closed his eyes. With a big exhale of air he drifted asleep. He would go back and check on his prisoner in a few days.

5

At twelve o' clock noon, McCabe waited at the tavern for George White Owl. He saw him pull up on the dock in a fishing boat. Greeting him at the dock, he chided him.

"How is your head this morning George?"

The Indian man groaned, "I am paying the price today. Tonight is another night though. How are your wounds?"

"They are a little sore but no big deal. They will heal. Do you want me to drive us over there?"

"No. I will be back in the tavern again tonight. We can take my boat."

They proceeded into Rice Bay and drove the boat several miles up the shoreline. The scenery was spectacular with large granite outcroppings towering above the waterline. An extremely rugged landscape was bordered by remote wilderness behind it for miles. Eventually they came to a small community of cabins along the shoreline on a sand beach. Several docks with boats tied to them formed a mini reservation marina.

"This is the reservation town of Raven," explained White Owl as he pulled the boat up. "About fifty residents from the reservation live in this bay. The others have cabins farther into the interior of the reservation. This is the town hall and community lodge, along with the homes of those who live here."

A gravel road ran through the group of log constructed buildings. "This road joins up to highway seven and the entrance to the reservation. Some of us even drive cars, too," he said sarcastically.

"It is good you were not driving last night," replied McCabe.

"I rarely leave the reservation when I am not working, except to go over to Flanagan's Resort. Even in the dark I know my way home from there by boat. I am an independent truck driver by trade. I drive mostly in the winter months. I own my own sixteen wheel semi truck."

"Well that is a comforting thought. I will remember that when I am driving down the interstate next time. What does your truck look like?, asked McCabe.

The Indian responded. "Not to worry Mr. McCabe. When I am working, I take my job very seriously. No drinking and driving. And I will be retiring in another year. I have had a clean driving record for twenty years and intend to keep it that way."

"Okay, well that's good." said McCabe chuckling. "Just a little drinking and boating I guess. Just be careful. You are on your own if something happened out there at night on the lake. I bet it would not be very easy to get help."

"I always am careful. You should do the same." He held up his radio transmitter. "On the lake the marine channel is our life line. Those rental boats at Flanagan's Resort don't have radios."

McCabe followed him around the back of the community log lodge to the back yard. There was a sweat lodge constructed of aspen poles covered with animal skins.

"This is an old tradition carried on mostly by the tribe elders. The sweat lodge has been considered a religious and inspirational place for centuries."

Within the lodge three Indian men sat in a circle around steaming rocks at the bottom of a dugout pit in the middle. Basically, it looked like a primitive sauna but it was extremely warm in there. Whatever they were doing it was working as a steam room.

A thermometer inside the lodge showed a temperature of one hundred twenty degrees. This was a visionary place for the old medicine men of Big Stone Reservation. An old man rocked back and forth in the wet heat, chanting in a Native American tongue.

The aged man began to speak in English as they sat down with him.

"The great eagle flew through the blue sky looking over the great forests and lakes. The eagle saw a huge man in the forest with many animals around him. The man held up his arm for the great bird to perch on. So the eagle swooped down and landed on his out-stretched arm. The man held the bird up to the sun and they were joined in spirit. On the forest floor, the powerful wolf appeared through the trees and lay at the man's feet. All three were joined in spirit to rule the forests and lakes and protect the land of the Indian."

The old Indian man fell backwards and stopped. "I must leave the heat of the lodge now."

White Owl and McCabe helped him out, each taking an arm.

"Some say the heat is too much for these old men and makes them crazy," said White Owl.

"This is my grandfather Ronald White Owl."

They helped him into a chair in the community center and gave him a cool drink. His grandson explained what had happened to McCabe yesterday. The very old man looked at McCabe.

"The legend says the curse would protect the reservation from the trespassing white man. The curse said a guardian of the reservation would come and protect the bay."

He continued on. "A giant man, not of Indian blood, would join in the universe with the spirit of the wolf and eagle. He would guard the land and kill his own people and spare no mercy. The man lives as one with the nature of the universe. He towered above the water with the eyes of the eagle and roams the boundaries where the water meets the forest. He has the stealth and cunning of the wolf. The great nature man was created by the curse to protect the Indian people from the encroaching white man."

The old man paused and sighed deeply.

"The chief vowed the curse would turn one of the white man's own people against them. This man would kill for fun as the men of 1949 did when they hung his son. It was the white man's nature to kill. The vengeance would be turned on them from within."

McCabe listened intently. Interesting, he thought, pondering the story.

The ancient man looked at McCabe.

"You may have been very near this great man spirit. Birds do not normally attack people. Tread carefully on Rice Bay. The dispute of 1949 was long ago. I am afraid the curse is forever."

George White Owl showed McCabe the rest of the community. He gave him a quick ride in a jeep and showed him the neighboring cabins. He swung by the reservation police station. A small building with a single squad car was parked outside.

"Here are my friends, the reservation police."

"Today, I will drive back to Flanagan's and avoid my police friends on the way home by boat."

"How many work there?"

"Just two cops, Police Chief Jerry Crow and his deputy Thomas Blackfoot. They don't do much. Break up domestics once in awhile and that's about it. They keep guys like me out of trouble when I drink too much."

A dirt road led out of the reservation for about seven miles. Then it joined to a tar road. White Owl turned right and just around the bend was the entrance to Flanagan's Resort.

He drove in and parked at the tavern. "Join me for a beer," asked White Owl. McCabe smiled and walked in with him. Flanagan approached them. "What will it be today, men?"
They ordered burgers and beer for lunch.

"My grandfather is wise but maybe a little crazy from the sweat lodge."

"Quite a story that's for sure," replied McCabe.

"There have been things over the years that have happened to people. Boating accidents and drowning victims for the most part. They were always explainable things. I don't know if I believe in the legend."

"Who knows, the old men seem to believe the curse," said McCabe. "Sometimes those old timers make sense of the unexplainable. Like your grandfather's mysterious spirit story."

"Yes, and maybe it makes unfortunate luck for some. I don't know anymore. I want to believe my elders but... I never see evidence. Maybe your bird attack was evidence of the curse."

McCabe patted White Owl's shoulder and stood up. "Many strange things happen in this world we live in. They probably just wanted to eat my fish. I thank you for the visit to meet your people. They live a good life in their quiet community."

"Most of the young men don't like it anymore. They want more night life and action. They think it is too remote a life style. My son and his friends moved off the reservation and live near Jackson. I hardly ever see them anymore."

McCabe wished White Owl well and walked out into the sunshine of the day. He didn't believe in spirits and ghosts and curses. He did believe in real people trying to make legends and curses come true though. There had been past murder cases of psychopathic copy cat killers trying to imitate a tall tale or urban legend.

As a federal officer, it was legal for him to investigate or talk to anyone he wanted to on the reservation. He didn't even need the approval of reservation police jurisdiction. As a courtesy he generally notified local authorities of what he was doing anyway.

He decided to phone the reservation police chief. He dialed him on his cell phone, explaining he was a federal agent investigating the Tanner's Lake murders. McCabe inquired if he had seen anything unusual this winter.

"Not a thing, sir. We are a very small community and I would know if something was going on. Somebody would know and gossip would spread. There are not really any secrets on the reservation."

"Okay, Thank you Chief Crow. I will stop by if my investigation leads to the north side of the lake and the reservation land."

McCabe spent the rest of the week talking to people in other resort bars. He drove twenty miles south to Windigo Resort and ate supper. This time he identified himself as an investigator and asked if anyone had seen anything unusual last winter.

He inquired if there was any open water on the lake in the winter time. The general answer was always no. He asked the question one more time to a bartender at the Windigo.

"I have never seen open water on this lake on December 1st. Usually it is completely frozen over for the winter season by Thanksgiving."

Another patron piped in at the bar. "I think those bodies got dumped in the lake at night through the ice. Someone must have cut a hole."

"What makes you think that?" said McCabe.

"I just don't see how they all got in there in the winter. Unless they got in there right before the lake froze."

"Who knows, but if you guys see or notice anything strange please contact Sheriff Campbell in Jackson. He can get in touch with me. I appreciate it."

McCabe finished his drink and left the tavern.

For several days he did the same thing. He questioned private cabin owners, asking if they saw anything strange last winter. One guy said he got in an argument with a guy on the north side who was walking out to his ice shack pulling a toboggan.

"He was a big dude pulling a toboggan across the lake at night. I almost hit him on my sled. I slowed down and told him he should have a flash light or reflective clothing on. He was wearing what looked like a parka made of animal skins."

"What did he say?"

"He said I should mind my own business and slow down. Not a very friendly guy at all. Then he picked up his fish spear and held it over his head like he was going to throw it or something. I just hit the gas and figured he was some drunken asshole going out to fish at night. There are plenty of them up here."

"Is that strange to go out at night spearing?"

"Sort off. You can't really see like the daytime because there is no sun. The water is dark. Some guys just fish out of them though at night. That can work pretty well."

"He was probably just going out to his shack to drink. It is probably just his home away from home like a lot of guys."

"Lots of drinking in those ice shacks?"

"Sure, a lot of guys go out and fish all night and drink beer. The nice ones have TV sets and bunks and everything. He may have had a couple of cases of beer loaded in that covered toboggan he was pulling."

"Where about did this happen?"

"I was up around Flanagan's Resort. I was going up there to see a few old friends from the Twin Cities staying at the resort."

"How far from Flanagan's place do you think?"

"I was cutting across the lake from the north east side off that state park land. My ice house is over on that side of the lake, not too far from the public landing. I pull it out from the landing at the start of the ice season. I keep it pretty close to the landing so it is not too hard to get off in the spring. The fishing is better on that side of the lake in the winter. It also gives me a good reason to open it up with my sled, living on the opposite side of the lake. That's the fun part."

McCabe wrote a couple of things in a notepad.

"What did this guy look like?"

"It was dark but what I remember was he was really big and had long black hair. No hat and some kind of animal skin parka. He looked kind of like a primitive guy or something. Like a man who had been in the woods for a very long time."

McCabe continued jotting notes.

"Okay, I appreciate the information. Probably nothing but so far that is all we have to this point. Maybe I can find someone who knows this guy."

"Well I hope you find whoever did this soon as it is giving everybody the creeps."

McCabe drove back to Flanagan's Resort wondering about the story of the big man on the ice. How could all these bodies get in the water through the ice? Maybe a guy like that wasn't going out for a night of fishing or drinking.

By week's end he had talked to about fifty people between Flanagan's Resort and the town of Jackson. Nobody really gave him much to go on. The one story about the big guy in animal skins kept bugging him.

Inside Flanagan's tavern, he sat once again with George White Owl and told the story he heard.

"Do you know any men who wear animal skins in the winter?"

"There are a few of the people on the reservation who still wear deer and bear skins. But none of them are big oversized men. Some drive to the public landing from Jackson and drive out on the lake when they can. Later in the year there is too much snow and you need to walk or snowmobile. Not much traffic once that happens."

"When does that usually happen where the snow is too deep to drive the lake?"

"Last year it happened on December 10th. We had a blizzard with about two feet of snow," replied White Owl.

McCabe pondered the resort patron's theory of bodies entering the lake through holes cut in the ice. Maybe they are right, he thought. His mind wandered back to his own situation on the investigation. With only two days left, he had hardly gone fishing since the first day when the birds attacked him. Tomorrow morning he was going fishing all day no matter what.

Once back in the office, he might not get back here until next fall or winter and only if this case remained unsolved. If he did get back here, he pondered what he might do.

Maybe he would rent a sled and take up ice fishing. Poke around a bit and get to know some of these ice fishermen. Or possibly do some fall bird hunting this season. Walk around that state forest by the landing with his bird dog looking for ruffed grouse.

Who knows, maybe he would stumble onto something. So far the killer was not making it easy and had not made contact with the press or police. Maybe he really was long gone just like Sheriff Campbell had thought.

6

Sheriff Campbell was originally alerted by Ben Thompson. The Cadwell brothers had now been missing for two days. They had rented a boat at Trapper's Cabins and had been fishing the lake all week. Thompson last saw them a week ago Monday.

After his weekend charter, they were out trying their luck by themselves. Thompson charged one hundred fifty dollars a day for his services. Usually his customers would go out on the first day or two of their trip and find the good fishing spots with the guide. Then they would venture out and catch fish all week.

That was exactly what they were doing last Monday when he saw them on his way back from Flanagan's Resort. The brothers said they had a good day fishing the north side.

The victim was barely alive when Thompson pulled up to the open boat. He thought the watercraft had drifted off someone's dock when he first spotted it unoccupied. It was a simple fishing boat, but the cargo it possessed was gruesome indeed. As he got closer the bow of the boat told the tale.

A skull was fixed about the anchor hoist, as bold as one could imagine. The naked body lying in the bottom of the boat was covered with dark grey blotches the size of corn kernels. Swollen red insect bites covered the man's body in every visible location. A human skeleton lay on the boat floor broken in pieces. Maggots still squirmed in the body cavity where small bits of flesh still remained.

Thompson nearly threw up at the sight. He anchored his boat and tied the floating vessel to his boat in order to stop the drift. He frantically grabbed his marine radio and called on the Sheriff's frequency.

"May Day, May Day. This is Ben Thompson."

"This is the Sheriff's office. Go ahead, Ben."

"We have a boat floating out here with two bodies in it. You got to get here right away. It's horrible. It's a skeleton."

"Are they alive?"

"I don't know. One could be. I think it might be Mike Cadwell from what I can see of his face. He is covered in grey stuff. I guided him and his brother about ten days ago. I know him. Please hurry."

"Roger that Ben, can you give me your GPS location."

Thompson read him the GPS coordinates from his depth finder. "I would say we are right about in the middle of the lake."

The Sheriff's boat roared across the lake and arrived in about fifteen minutes. As the boat linked up next to the floating nightmare, the men were shocked.

Sheriff Campbell had been in law enforcement for over thirty years and lived through vicious combat in the Vietnam war. He was generally not amazed at anything concerning blood and gore, but this was a gruesome sight indeed.

The skeleton draped across the bow of the boat appeared to be nearly whole. It almost looked like it had come from a doctor's office except for one obvious distinction. It was clear this skeleton was very real with a few squirming maggot's still feeding.

"My God, what has happened here?" exclaimed Campbell. His deputy Randy Baker stared at the skeleton silently until a moan from the other body brought both officers to action.

"That one is still alive!" shouted Baker.

Sheriff Campbell grabbed a canvas boat tarp and a strap board used for victims with spinal cord injuries. "Let's get him in our boat and get him back to the hospital."

He jumped in the boat and covered the skeleton in front with a canvas tarp. The two officers carefully lifted the injured man from both sides onto the board in one fluid motion, while Thompson supported his head.

When they strapped him down they realized what was covering his body. It was a common sight in the spring on local dogs in the area. Fat blood engorged wood ticks were showing a sick grey color. As they tightened the strap board, several ticks fell off his body with tiny feet wiggling below their obese bodies.

"Jesus, he's covered with wood ticks," said Campbell disgustedly.

The two men lifted the board across to the police cuddy cabin style boat. The rocking boats made this maneuver difficult, but the man's condition left no time to tow him in or wait for additional support.

Campbell grabbed a spare anchor and tied it to the fishing boat with the covered skeleton. He ordered his deputy to stay with the boat until he returned.

"Don't touch anything else and don't try to start the motor and drive it in. We will tow it to the garage. If anyone comes by keep them off. We will be back in about fifteen minutes."

He locked in their GPS position and started the cruiser.

Grabbing a pair of gloves, he threw them to the deputy. "Put these on and try not to disturb anything. We want photographs before we tow this thing in."

Deputy Baker did not seem thrilled with his new assignment babysitting a dead guy. "Just hurry back. This gives me the creeps sitting out here like this."

"Keep your eyes open. I will be back in forty five minutes or less. Ben, can you follow me in back to the docks? We will need your report on this whole thing."

His tone sounded odd to Thompson. Almost like he was implying he had something to do with it.

"No problem, Sheriff. I'll be right behind you."

Campbell hit the throttle and the big twenty four foot Sheriff's cruiser with twin one hundred fifty horse power engines clipped across the big lake cutting waves.

Thompson's guide boat was probably even faster and kept pace, no problem. It was built to move where the fish were biting fast. For his high priced guiding fees, he didn't waste much time getting to the fishing spots.

The victim lay covered in the cuddy cabin below in the Sheriff's Cruiser. Getting on his marine radio he called the police station. "May Day, May Day, this is Campbell over."

One of his deputies responded. "I copy that, Sheriff, go ahead, over."

"I have an emergency situation on the lake. I am bringing in a critically injured man by boat. I need an ambulance at the South Shore landing in about fifteen minutes. Repeat, situation is critical with victim unconscious, shallow breathing and weak pulse. He has probably lost a lot of blood as well. We will be there in fifteen minutes. See you at the docks."

"Copy, we will be ready for transport on arrival, over and out."

As the cruiser slowed to the town docks the paramedics were waiting. Three medics jumped in the boat and transferred the body board to a wheeled gurney on the pier. Another prepared an IV in the ambulance and looked for a spot to insert the needle.

The driver closed the double doors on the back and ran to the wheel. In moments the ambulance was completely gone from sight.

Campbell's thoughts returned to the situation on the lake. He spoke to one of his uniformed officers.

"We need a sixteen foot boat trailer down here from the garage. We have another dead victim adrift in a boat. I'm going back out for evidence photos and then towing it in. We will be back here as quick as we can. Rope this area off from the public. The landing is closed until we get back. Have the trailer in the water when we get here. Thanks."

Campbell turned around as he was walking to his boat.

"Oh, and can you take Ben up to the office and have him wait for me. I want to talk to him right when I get back."

He looked at Ben.

"You don't mind waiting do you Ben?"

Thompson shook his head no and went with the officer. "I would rather go along with you though."

"Sorry Ben. This is strictly police business at this point. This is a homicide investigation. I need to talk to you about anything you might have seen on the lake today."

The Sheriff picked up his cell phone and made a call to their forensic team. He instructed them to impound the boat and store it in the police garage awaiting further investigation. The FBI would be doing the evidence work. With that he untied the police boat and began the journey back to the crime scene.

Deputy Baker sat in the small boat staring at the tarp draping the bow. A strange silence fell over the lake as the big boats disappeared from view at high speed. The small foot bones of the skeleton poked out from under the tarp. He wondered what could have happened to these people. The howl of a timber wolf to the north echoed a lonely cry across the water.

He looked around the boat and noticed the minnow bucket on the floor. Looking inside, the dead minnows were fat and bloated as if they had died some time ago. The fattened wood ticks that had fallen from the body were trying to crawl up the side of the boat and sliding back down.

He remembered Sheriff Campbell's orders. Wear the gloves and don't touch anything. The minutes passed like hours as he sat alone on the lake with the covered corpse. Not a boat in sight as the waves rocked the little boat.

After a few minutes a boat appeared on the west side of the lake headed his way. The boat approached slowly and when it was about one hundred yards away it turned directly towards him. As it approached the driver waved and pulled up next to him. He recognized investigator McCabe as the boat pulled up and felt a sigh of relief.

"I picked up the radio transmissions from my truck."

McCabe flashed his identification badge in formality.

"What have we got here?

Deputy Baker looked at him sternly. "You don't want to know."

He folded the tarp on the skeleton back, providing McCabe a quick peek at the corpse.

"Holy shit," exclaimed McCabe.

He dropped his boat anchor about ten feet away and waited for Sheriff Campbell to return. "Any idea what happened?"

Baker shook his head. "We might find out though. There was another guy covered in wood ticks that was still barely alive. Maybe he can tell us."

"I hope so, because I have not turned up much yet, that's for sure." He pulled out a small digital camera and took some pictures of the boat. "Can you pull that tarp back again for me?"

Sheriff Campbell's boat appeared on the horizon speeding toward them. As he glided up to the boat he grabbed a tow rope and threw it to his deputy.

He looked at McCabe floating next to him. "What happened to you?" looking at his cut up face. "Somebody at Flanagan's bar kick your ass?"

"You are a funny guy, Sheriff. Got this murder solved for me yet? This is more than likely related to last winter."

"What makes you think that hot shot?"

"The skeleton does not have any teeth. It's the serial killer's signature."

Campbell was feeling the stress of the situation. He had seen skeletons in Viet Nam. It was not a pleasant memory.

"I want to talk to you when we get back. We're going to tow the whole rig into the garage and have it dusted for prints. We best not find any of your prints in the boat or you might have an extended stay on Tanner's Lake." Deputy Baker grabbed the tow line and tied it off at the bow.

"Take it easy Jason, he kept his hands off. He picked us up on his radio and came over to help. I showed him the skeleton."

McCabe just shook his head. The FBI had complete authority on this case if he ordered it. He wanted to work with the local police because they were valuable to him. They knew the area and had the equipment and connections he needed to work this case.

He figured they were just upset with the disturbing gruesomeness of it all. As a serial murder investigator, he had seen some pretty bad things in the past.

"I will meet you guys back at the station. I am going back to my truck and driving into town. It is too far for this small boat to go all the way to the south side of the lake."

He started the motor and looked at Sheriff Campbell.

"Try not to touch any potential evidence before I get there. I will be doing the print dusting personally on this one."

He hit the throttle and pointed the boat back to the resort. Tying his boat up to one of Flanagan's docks, he hustled into his cabin to grab a few items. From his suitcase he pulled out a pair of gloves, plastic baggies, tweezers, a video camera, and a compact tape recorder.

Jumping into his truck he headed toward Jackson, wondering if the other victim had died. As he turned on the main highway he put on his red dash light and sounded his siren.

Instead of driving into town, he turned east at high speed racing towards the hospital. I need to talk to him before it is too late, he thought. Entering the hospital parking lot he skidded to a stop. At the reception desk he was greeted by a petite young woman.

Showing his badge he inquired if an accident victim had been brought in from Tanner's Lake in the past hour. "Do you have the name of the patient, Mr. McCabe?"

"No. He was unconscious and had no identification. As a matter of fact, he had no clothing."

The woman looked through the admitting records for the day.

"We have an unidentified critical male in the intensive care unit. It looks like he was admitted to surgery about a half hour ago."

McCabe nodded, "That sounds like the guy. I need to see him, it is extremely important."

The receptionist shook her head. "He is in intensive care and can't see visitors. I am sorry Mr. McCabe but you will need to wait until he is better."

McCabe wasted no time. He walked through the double doors where the patients are admitted and began looking for the intensive care unit.

The receptionist followed him through the doors, ordering him to stop. He glared at the woman and stopped her in her tracks.

"You could be indicted for hampering a murder investigation if he dies before I can speak to him."

She gave in immediately. "ICU is down the hall to the right. I am very sorry. I am just doing what I was told."

When he saw the man he could hardly believe his eyes. The doctors were removing the wood ticks into a plastic bucket. The man's eyes were wide open in a glazed stare.

McCabe held his badge up to the doctors. "Federal Officer McCabe, homicide unit. Can I speak to him? We have reason to believe this could be connected to the Tanner's Lake murders."

One of the doctors pulled him aside to the hallway area.

"First, he is in a deep state of shock. And second, you need a mask and gown to go in there."

McCabe acknowledged, "I understand, can I observe? It could be important."

The doctor directed him to a nurse who supplied him with a cap, gown and mask.

"Is he going to make it, doc?"

The doctor looked at him gravely serious.

"He is stable right now as far as body sign vitals go. Unfortunately, his state of shock is so severe it's hard to say what will happen to his mind."

In the pre-operating room, four doctors finished removing the last of the swollen ticks. The man's skin was covered with red raw bites from head to toe.

"Infection from these bites could be a problem. He has serious skin damage and loss of blood from the exceptional number of bites. He also had a body temperature of ninety two degrees when admitted and was hypothermic."

McCabe motioned to a nurse removing the ticks in two plastic containers.

"Don't dispose of them. We may need this as evidence and the count that were removed. He didn't get that many from just being out in the woods. Somebody must have put those on him. Can you freeze them and our FBI evidence team will pick them up later?"

The nurse nodded in acknowledgement. The doctors moved the man to the next room for a series of x-rays. The victim's eyes remained wide open in a blank stare as they moved him to the next room. He attempted to speak as the gurney was pushed past McCabe.

He bent over him with the microphone from his tape recorder clipped to his shirt collar. The man gurgled in a barely audible noise attempting to speak.

"Take it easy fellah, did someone do this to you?"

Tears flowed from the man's eyes as his mouth struggled to move. He moved his head forward and groaned "RIICCEEEE BAAAYYYY." McCabe could not understand him.

The doctors intervened as his heart monitor jumped dramatically. "Alright, that's it. Stabilizing the patient with two milligrams of morphine."

The doctor injected him with the needle and he closed his eyes. The heart monitor returned to normal again.

"Get some x-rays on this guy fast and let's see what is going on inside."

The doctor turned to McCabe. "I can't let that happen again."

McCabe nodded, "Okay, I understand."

"If we can stabilize him enough to where he can talk, you will be the first to know. Give the nurse your number."

He wrote his cell number on the back of his card and handed it to her. "I am staying on Tanner's Lake. Can I call you tomorrow and see how he is doing?"

"We will know more about his condition, but I can't say you will be able to talk to him. I can't say if he will be alive. Right now his condition is class nine ICU critical. About seventy percent of patients in that category don't make it past twenty four hours."

The doctor handed him his card. "Call me tomorrow. I will give you a personal reading on his condition. I assure you we will do everything we can to keep him alive."

McCabe took the card and nodded as the patient came out of x-ray and a team of doctors rushed him over to surgery.

"Thanks."

He left the hospital and in the cab of his truck he played the tape recording. "What is he trying to say?"

He shook his head and started the engine. When he arrived at Sheriff Campbell's office, a forensic team had just removed the skeleton. Campbell approached McCabe.

"We decided to let you dust the boat for prints. You have the most training in that area. Sorry about my crack on the boat. I just don't need anyone getting carried away until we decide how we want to handle this thing."

McCabe glared at him as the general attitude was beginning to annoy him. He decided to let Campbell know how the FBI works.

"Local jurisdiction doesn't mean shit in a national murder case of this size. I have reason to believe this is linked to your spring body surfing extravaganza, so back off. I appreciate you waiting for me, but you might not have a job anymore if you didn't. Especially since I told you I would do it."

"Your apology is accepted if you took photographs before removing the dead guy from the boat." McCabe looked at Campbell inquisitively listening for a response.

"You did get pictures of the crime scene didn't you?"

"Don't worry hot shot. We had our photographer take pictures. Let's see you do your stuff. And by the way, I might have to work with you, but I don't have to like you."

McCabe smiled and replied sarcastically.

"Don't hurt my feelings Sheriff. I am a sensitive guy. Besides, we may like working together before this is over. I might become a permanent resident and you can take me out on that big boat of yours. Maybe I can even wear a police uniform."

McCabe photographed the boat again for a second time. He had shots when it was on the water as well. Any potential evidence was bagged in plastic and the boat was dusted with powder. One of the prints came from the bow near the printed letters, Trapper's Cabins.

"Have you spoken to the owners of this place yet?"

Campbell nodded, "They reported a boat and a couple of customers missing without settling up their final bill about three days ago."

"Who are they?"

"They were checked in as Mike and Jim Cadwell. Apparently they were brothers. At least that is what they said at check in. They were staying there for ten days." He continued on. "We did an air search and couldn't spot the boat so we had no reason to think they drowned. We didn't know what to think, so we put out a DNR and Forestry alert to be on the lookout for them.

Ben Thompson described them as young and kind of wild. First, we thought they might have stolen the boat and hauled it out on a public landing. Their vehicle is still at the resort though."

He looked over at Ben Thompson still in the office.

"Ben didn't think so either. Not the stealing type, just good paying customers and fun guys. He thought it was more likely they might have taken off on some wild adventure. Maybe portaged the boat to another lake. People can disappear in these woods."

"We did everything other than a full blown search with dogs. Aluminum fishing boats of that type do not sink. It should have floated up on shore somewhere. There are nine hundred miles of shoreline on this lake system. We couldn't walk the whole thing with a couple of blood hounds."

McCabe shook his head. "That's a hell of a long time to be reported missing without a full blown search. Did you run a plate check on the vehicles and notify relatives?"

Deputy Baker jumped into the conversation. "We didn't want to alarm anyone yet. They had the cabin for over a week. We figured they would show up."

"So we really don't even know when they officially went missing?"

"The cabin owners had not seen them for the last several days they had the place rented. So potentially about seven to ten days," said Campbell.

McCabe placed his hand on his forehead. "Well I must say they sure showed up in style. Look, it probably wouldn't have mattered anyway. At least, not to the victim who was reduced to a skeleton. The other guy probably would have been thrilled about a full blown search party."

Sheriff Campbell protected their work. "That's enough McCabe. When you learn these parts better come back and see me. Then I'll have a much better opinion of your judgment concerning tracking people who get lost around here. We do about ten search and rescues per season on average."

McCabe shrugged and kept his mouth shut momentarily and continued dusting the boat for prints.

Two separate prints were found on the boat. Two unusually large palm prints and a thumb print were found. Both were located near the bow of the boat. Another print was found near where the second hospitalized man was located.

McCabe took close up photographs of all the prints and ordered Sheriff Campbell to impound the boat. Next he asked Campbell to finger print everyone who had contact with the boat.

Campbell balked at the idea and glared at him. "Are you insinuating that one of my men was involved?"

"Absolutely not, I need to rule out everyone including the forensic team."

"Understandable, but wouldn't that turn up on the BCA report?"

"All my people are finger printed before they can work here."

"That is a good point and it is quite true, however, it costs money and takes time to run those scans. It is better to rule it out now," responded McCabe.

"I really don't want to put my people through that."

"I can tell my boss that, and he will probably call you and ask why you have delayed a national print check on the only damn lead we have in this case. He won't send those prints through unless we know they don't come from the people investigating the case."

"The press gets hold of that and next they are asking why it is taking us so long. Pretty soon they say we are wasting taxpayer's money and mishandling evidence. We don't need any embarrassments in this case. It's really nothing personal, it is standard procedure."

Campbell complied grudgingly after such a convincing argument. "No problem, you made your point. I still hate to ask everyone as they will think we are investigating staff."

"Explain it to them and they won't. That's your job."

"Maybe I will talk to Captain Becker, your boss, and see if he can put someone on this case who thinks a little more like we do. You may think we are just a bunch of small town hick cops that write speeding tickets, but that's where you're wrong.

Everyone on my staff is well trained and has worked in big cities in the past. Except me, I got my start as an MP at Fort

Bragg, so I have dealt with a lot of young smart ass guys like you."

"That's good. Then you should know all about following orders from superior jurisdictions. Like the FBI for example."

McCabe pulled out his ink blotter and print pads from his brief case. "You can request whatever you damn please, and I wish you luck. You will need it."

As Sheriff Campbell was printed McCabe made small talk.

"So, I understand it is an election year this fall in Jackson County. Bet you're not looking forward to that if this case is still unsolved." Campbell poured a cup of coffee and walked away mumbling inaudible comments. McCabe finished the last print on one of the forensic guys.

"Thanks gentlemen. I will be leaving town in the morning after I speak with Ben Thompson and the paramedics. Hopefully, our patient at the hospital will be feeling better tomorrow and can enlighten us on this psychotic son of a bitch. He didn't look to hot a couple of hours ago."

The patients x-rays showed why his pain was so immense. The tick bites and emaciated condition were a problem, but it really should not kill a person if the infection was controlled. When McCabe spoke to the doctor he was once again shocked by the brutality.

"So what can you tell me doctor?"

"Unfortunately, our patient did not survive the night. He went into shock and died last night."

McCabe was obviously disappointed. "No……was there a specific cause of death?"

"There was physical trauma, shock and a number of other factors that contributed to his death. But the main cause of death was a swelling of the brain due to infection."

"The x-rays revealed a sharp object had been inserted up the patient's nose creating a small hole to the brain. It almost looked like a rudimentary lobotomy had been performed. There was tissue damage to the frontal brain lobes. We also discovered biting black ants had entered the cranial cavity via the puncture and were feeding. The resulting trauma to the brain killed him. We believe the other body found with him was stripped of flesh by ants and maggots as well. I'm sorry agent McCabe."

McCabe put his hand to his forehead. "Jesus, were you able to come up with anything we can use to identify them for sure?"

"The coroner is working on this now. Our patients teeth were gone as were the other victim's as well. They are doing full body x-rays on the cadavers, looking for old breaks that can prove they might be somebody who is missing. Ben Thompson identified this one as Mike Cadwell, one of his fishing clients. Good chance the other one is his brother as they are both reported missing."

The doctor continued to explain further.

"We can verify they are brothers through DNA testing against his potentially unidentifiable brother. In court we generally need the DNA anyway, so in a case like this, I have already ordered DNA testing. It is expensive but it will also screen for anyone else's DNA on the bodies.

We are already working with a forensic expert from the FBI instructing us on what tests we need to do. Your boss, FBI Captain Becker, apparently saw this unfold on the news and sent down a forensic team."

McCabe had actually phoned Becker on his way to the hospital that morning. "Excellent. That is a wise idea. How long will the tests take?"

"Normally, we can tell you by the end of the week. We need to talk to their families for approval. Generally, it is not a problem, as they want to catch the criminal more than anyone."

"Thanks, Doctor. Please let me know when the results of the tests are in. Here is my card".

McCabe dropped the phone and put his hand to his forehead thinking. What kind of sick bastard would do such a thing to another human being?

It was obviously tied to the Tanner's Lake murders of last winter. Missing teeth on the victims was an obvious signature statement. The serial killer was back in business in the Tanner's

Lake neighborhood. In the morning, prints were taken from Ben Thompson and the paramedics. Thompson was saddened by the death of his friends and former clients.

McCabe did not share all the grisly details in an effort to ease the tension. He was aware of the fact that Thompson was around the discovery of victims from the get go.

First, there was the initial discovery in the ice shack. Then second, the discovery of a boat adrift with more victims six months later. Probably nothing, but he needed to be observant and aware of it. He had handled enough murder cases to know anything was possible. Thompson had to be considered as a possible suspect. It would not be the first time a victim knew and trusted their killer.

All the prints gathered from the Sheriff's staff were different than the large thumb print at the bow of the boat. The print was in a position to suggest it may have been pushing the boat off and setting it adrift.

During his observations from a week at Flanagan's Resort, the wind and waves were always moving north to south. Maybe that was why most of the bodies were discovered on the south shore as well.

McCabe drove back to his home office to run the thumb and palm prints against the national database. The two hour drive back to the office gave him plenty of time to think.

Possibly the large print was made by the killer pushing the boat adrift. Mike and Jim Cadwell appeared to be just two fun loving brothers who were apparently in the wrong place at the right time for the killer.

Many people on the FBI missing person's list met the size descriptions of the bodies recovered on Tanner's Lake. Unfortunately, there were no positive links based on hard facts such as finger prints or dental records.

The best lead he had was a potential matching case record for a missing female from Texas. She was a known prostitute with a badly broken and pinned left femur as a child. Currently, it was feared she was a victim in an ongoing serial murder investigation in San Antonio. The River Walk murders were being investigated by another FBI team.

The only female Caucasian body discovered on Tanner's Lake had a left femur that been broken badly and pinned long ago. It was a long shot but worthy of further investigation. The missing woman disappeared last winter in San Antonio. The bone size correlated with a bone from Tanner's Lake for approximate length and structure.

They could test the bone DNA to see if it matched any of her relatives. Sixteen prostitutes had been murdered so far in the River Walk murders. He knew the primary female investigator working the case quite well. Over the years, he had attended several FBI training classes with her. In their last class together about nine months ago, they were teammates in a mock serial investigation.

McCabe met with Captain Becker to brief him on the case.

"I think it is a very high probability that the Caldwell brothers were killed by the same person who killed everyone else. Unless we have a copycat killer operating now, I would say it is about 99.9% for sure. For one thing, the missing teeth signature was apparent on both bodies. Looks like more souvenirs for our killer."

Captain Becker reviewed the photographs of the case as McCabe spoke.

"Before Cadwell died, he tried to tell me something. When I asked him if someone did this to him he nodded and said this."

He played the tape for him.

"What did he say?"

"I am not sure, but it almost sounds like he was saying the name of a bay on Tanner's Lake".

McCabe plugged the recorder into a larger stereo receiver and played it again. "Listen closely when I speed it up and amplify it."

Becker listened intently and spoke aloud. "Sounds like he is saying raceway?"

"Maybe, but I don't think so. There is also a Rice Bay on the lake."

"Is there a race track up there?"

"Yeah, there is a dirt track about ten miles out of town. And I checked out the background on the brothers and they liked fast cars. They did go to the races once in awhile too according to their sister. I think it might be worth sending someone up to Jackson speedway to ask around if anyone saw them at the track recently."

Becker stared at the photos of both bodies. "I really want to nail this psycho. You got anything else?"

McCabe smiled, "I got a couple of prints off the boat. One was a decent thumb print and two large palm prints. Whoever it is, they have big hands. I am running them through the BCA database right now on a national check. I also printed the local authorities who may have touched the boat accidentally while loading it, like Sheriff Campbell and his deputies."

McCabe laughed slightly. "It really pissed him off as he was wearing gloves the whole time. I printed the resort owner and everyone else involved, with no match as well."

Captain Becker smiled, "You always did know how to improve relations with the local authorities. What the hell, I agree with you. You have to make sure. Especially if that print does belong to a convicted felon. This case is too big to worry about stepping on toes. Do what you have to do."

McCabe grinned. "I've got more, but this one I need a favor from you. I went over the forensic file with a fine tooth comb looking for links to the national missing person's database. I made about fifty phone calls around the county to family members with one question about their missing loved ones."

"Did she ever have a broken left leg as a child?"

"Where are you going with this McCabe?"

"One of the bodies last winter was a female Caucasian with a broken pinned left femur. I discovered that a missing hooker down in San Antonio who was briefly investigated as a potential victim on the River Walk case, also had a broken left leg. She is white and the broken leg was pinned as a child. I think we should go down there and see if the bones match up. The relatives have already said they would cooperate and let me pull the medical file and x-rays."

Captain Becker thought for a moment. "Like I said earlier, do what you think you need to do on this one. Whoever is doing this is not going to stop until we catch them."

McCabe nodded his head in agreement.

"I know Federal Agent Montgomery working on the case down there too. If this matches up, she would be very interested to say the least. Maybe the cases are somehow connected."

Becker looked up and smiled knowingly at his top investigator.

"I know her too, and she is a pretty attractive lady. I am sure that has nothing to do with it though. Get down there and get me something on this case."

"Okay boss. I'm on it."

McCabe bolted out the door before he changed his mind. Okay, bring it on San Antonio, he thought to himself as he hurried home to pack. It would be nice to see Shelly Montgomery again.

7

The plane skidded to the runway, slowing to a stop at San Antonio airport. McCabe grabbed his carry on luggage and departed the airplane. A busy Monday morning in the terminal, he was glad he only had carry on luggage.

He picked up his nine millimeter government issued revolver from a special federal security weapons pickup window. Next he stopped at the rental car booth and rented a car. An attractive young lady wrote him a contract for a 2009 Dodge Charger.

Walking outside from the air conditioning, the heat was intense even in May. He saw his car sitting at the edge of the lot. It was a four door car, with a hemi engine and chrome wheels. Jet black in color, it looked very sharp.

He threw his bag in the back seat and climbed in the car. Pulling out his mobile computer phone, he prepared to make a call. Punching up his contacts on the cell phone, he opened Shelly Montgomery's address listing and dialed. A woman answered. "Homicide, can I help you?"

"Is Shelly Montgomery available?"

"This is Shelly."

"Hi Shelly, this is Jack McCabe from Minneapolis. Remember me from our evidence class?"

She smiled. "Jack, how could I forget a memorable week studying with the likes of you?"

"I was told you would be contacting me today. How was your flight?"

"It was great. We didn't crash which is always a plus in my book."

"Still have the sense of humor I see. Do you know how to get to the Federal Building in San Antonio?"

"No, but I have a map. I will see you in about eight hours. Just kidding but you know how I get lost. Hopefully traffic will not be too bad."

She shook her head remembering. "It should take about thirty minutes to get here. That is, if you take the right way which is probably unlikely in your case."

"I will see you in about a half hour Miss Montgomery. I am looking forward to working with you again."

McCabe briefly reviewed the city map on his computerized phone. She doesn't know I have an electronic map these days, he thought.

Almost immediately his car was stopped in a traffic jam. He finally arrived at the Federal Building about a half hour late. As he passed through the doors of the Federal Building, security guards checked his identification. He was escorted up to the homicide unit by one of the guards.

Speaking through a glass window with a clerk, he asked to see Shelly Montgomery.

"One moment please."

The locked office door buzzed opened to a pretty professional looking woman of Hispanic descent. She had dark long hair and wore an attractive skirt with a revolver clipped to the belt.

She smiled and held out her hand to McCabe. "Nice to see you again, Jack. I thought you might call me sometime after the class."

He shook her hand and entered her office. "Uh, yeah… I meant to call, but you know how it is with long distance relationships. Just makes it hard on everyone."

She laughed seductively. "Yeah, I wouldn't want to make it hard on you Jack."

They appeared to have gotten to know each other pretty well in the past from her tone of voice.

"That's okay, don't worry about it."

Shelly had grown up in south Texas and started her career in law enforcement as a young Federal Border Patrol agent. It was very dangerous work with the emerging drug cartels moving from Juarez into El Paso. The government had officially called the violence spillover, as the murders and gang fighting increased every year into the United States. Shelly built a reputation as a tough, smart young lady that could handle herself in most any situation. Eventually, the FBI decided to promote her and move her to a homicide unit in Dallas which specialized in serial murder investigations. Her superiors thought she was getting too well known and wanted to take her out of harm's way. She was much too valuable and talented for them to risk losing her service forever.

The gangs were murdering Mexican police on a regular basis. Because she was of Hispanic decent herself, she was even more of a target than many of the other agents. She was responsible for a number of drug trafficking arrests and was assisting the El Paso police who were diligently trying to stop, or at least slow down, the major drug cartels operating across the border. Drugs were being moved into the United States at an alarming rate and the violence was right behind it. It was slowly becoming a war zone with thousands of murders per year in the small metropolitan area. Each year it seemed to get a little worse. Many innocent people were dying in retaliation killings by the cartels. The Mexican government had basically declared war on the Juarez cartels who were not taking it lying down. Many of the Mexican police were dead or they quit as it was just too dangerous of a job. Some believed military assistance might someday be needed to stop the carnage. Shelly was glad she got out in the earlier years before the violence became totally out of control. She probably would be dead by now had she continued to arrest the gang members of El Paso on a regular basis.

Her new job had made her develop a whole new set of skills to track serial murders. She had been working the homicide unit about four years now, and found it challenging and interesting. She was the chief investigator on the San Antonio River Walk murders and was determined to catch the criminal.

Serial killers were usually very elusive, intelligent and could blend into society. It was much different than dealing with drug trafficking, which was usually all about money and gangs. The serial killer profile could be almost anyone. Most of the time it was an individual nobody even suspected. Someone the neighbor would often say was a quiet nice person who kept to himself.

She had cracked a major case in New Orleans two years prior. This was a killer working the French Quarter district abducting and killing male and female bar patrons returning home on foot. The killer was a white male who was angry with local and federal authorities over how hurricane Katrina had been handled. He blamed them for the terrible suffering many underwent during the delayed evacuations and relief help. He also enjoyed killing for sport and believed he was getting revenge on the police by disrupting their operations and putting fear into the community.

Basically, the killer wanted to make authorities look bad on unsolved murders that were beginning to mount. The more he killed, the more fear it put into the community and the more pressure on the police to solve the case. That was the payback he was seeking and his lack of conscience made the victims simply necessary collateral damage to attain his desired result.

Shelly managed to catch him on his seventeenth murder attempt. The killer had been taunting the police and vowed he would strike again within forty eight hours. Shelly went undercover and used herself as bait, posing as an intoxicated female wandering home from the bar district alone late at night. She had been stumbling along the sidewalk next to a French Quarter cemetery singing and talking to herself. She had doused herself with whisky to play the role and was still drinking a Hurricane as she rested near the open cemetery gate entrance.

The cemetery was a featured spot of several ghost touring companies in town. A man approached her from inside the cemetery gates, asking if she needed help getting home. First she wondered if he might have been lost on a ghost tour that had gone through the cemetery about an hour earlier. That seemed unlikely as the tour guide generally led the group with a flashlight telling scary stories about the entombed residents. It would be hard to lose the entire group. She said she did need a little help and asked him drunkenly if he would walk her to her hotel. He asked her where she was staying and she gave him an address about six blocks away on the other side of the cemetery.

The man suggested a shortcut through the cemetery as he had just come from that way. He knew the hotel she was staying at and told her it was a much shorter walk, especially for someone in her condition. She balked at the idea just to see how he would react. If she just instantly agreed to it, she might seem like a baited plant and scare him off. He claimed to be an off duty cop and flashed a badge at her. He said he just wanted to see her home safely as it could be a dangerous place at night.

Shelly took the bait and reluctantly agreed since he was a cop. She began to move through the dark cemetery leaning on him for support. When they were into the cemetery about fifty yards he started talking weird. He started talking about dead people and asked her if she ever wondered what it would be like to be dead. His hand began to tighten on her right arm, slowly gripping it harder and harder. He asked her if she liked cops and if she liked him. She wasn't sure how to respond so she said she had never met one before. Then he said he hated cops and sometimes pretended to be a cop just to do bad things. At that point he suddenly just attacked her. He put a knife to her throat and dragged her behind a large cement family sarcophagus. She was lucky he didn't slash her throat immediately. She acknowledged she was a cop as he dragged her away and he decided to terrorize her before killing her. He told her she would be his seventeenth victim, and the most gratifying if she was in fact a cop. He thought it could really make the police look bad if he killed one of their own members. Especially after warning them he would kill again in the next forty eight hours.

He removed her gun from under her open coat shoulder harness before she could get to it. He told her he was going to cut her ears off and send them to the local police. He demanded her name and threw her on the ground pointing the pistol in her face. The full moon threw a soft dim light on his figure as he moved. Digging through her purse he found her FBI credentials using a pen light for illumination. Shelly seized the opportunity as he was distracted for a split second reading the ID.

She held a third degree black belt in karate and also had another weapon strapped to her thigh. She hit him in the throat with her right hand and simultaneously knocked the gun up and away from her with her left hand. As she did so the gun went off, narrowly missing her. She followed up with an elbow to the face knocking him backwards causing him to drop the gun. He lunged at her with his knife, but she had her backup piece already drawn. She shot him once in the upper left shoulder area and then physically disarmed him and made the arrest. She brought him in alive and he made a full confession. Once again, she showed the fearless attitude she often displayed in El Paso to get the job done one way or another. It was risky baiting yourself to a killer but it worked this time.

Shelly had taken several serial killer profile courses with Jack in the past. He also attended yearly mandatory risk assessment training with her. Those courses were designed to help you make the right decisions and stay alive when under attack or distress.

Shelly was assigned to the FBI's south central serial investigation unit. Jack was in the north central division. There were four other divisions located on the east and west coasts. Each division would move to wherever the crime was occurring within their respective area and set up investigative operations. They were highly trained and knew what to look for and what to expect from a serial killer. It was unusual for them to cross into other divisions on an active investigation, but sometimes it was necessary if the killer was on the move. Shelly got down to business with Jack McCabe right away.

"What have you got going in Minneapolis that brings you to San Antonio?"

"What would you say if I had a possible physical link to the River Walk murders?"

"I would say wow! The case has been cold for about nine months now."

"Well, maybe it is cold because your killer is working in the Minnesota winters. Have you heard of the Tanner's Lake murders yet?"

"Briefly, from what I have heard, it is a gory affair of bodies turning up on a big lake."

"That's putting it mildly. We have a real psycho on the loose in this one. Anyhow, of all the body parts we have found, I could have a match to a missing hooker in the River Walk case."

"Which one are you looking at?"

"Denise Williams. I have a broken left femur and her relatives tell me she had one too. I need to check the medical records for a match."

"That is kind of a long shot Jack."

"Yeah it is, but it's something we need to check. Plus it gives me the opportunity to visit you in person. The heck with phone calls to you, I need to see you in the flesh."

His charm made her shut the office door. She moved near him and ran her finger down his tie. "Where are you staying tonight Jack? Maybe we can go out to dinner?"

"I would love to Miss Montgomery. I thought you would never ask." She led him down a corridor to a large room with photographs pinned up on a cork board.

"These are the known murdered victims from the River Walk file. We have a sadistic killer on the loose too. From what I have heard in a briefing from a cross case investigator, they don't link up though. This case has strangled and stabbed hookers, some beaten to death. Your case has body parts and missing teeth. It doesn't sound like the same killer."

"You might be right on different killers. Our latest victim had vicious torture as well. We have to follow up on everything before this case goes cold like River Walk."

"Someone in the northern bush country is killing people and then getting rid of them in the lake. It appears they were dumped before the ice went out. Who knows how many more bodies might be out there in the woods somewhere. This case could be huge if we can break it open."

She was not familiar with ice on lakes, but nodded in agreement.

"Okay, what do you need to know about the River Walk case?"

McCabe showed her a printed picture of Denise Williams which he had obtained from her family via email.

"Have you ever seen or heard of her?"

"Denise Williams, a missing hooker who had been arrested numerous times in San Antonio for prostitution. We thought she could be linked to the case, but we found the bodies of all the others. Not only did we find them, they were put on display by the killer. He would dress them up in real nice clothes and then dump the bodies."

Here is the file on the investigation. McCabe paged through the photographs and notes.

"We thought Denise Williams had probably gone straight or was not working the area anymore. She has really not been a part of the River Walk case to this point. She disappeared about the time we found our last body. Maybe it could be something if he changed his methods on the rest of the killings."

McCabe nodded, "One other thing. We picked up finger prints from our last victims. We are running a check through the BCA national database. Has your investigation turned up any prints?"

"Unfortunately our killer does very clean work. Apparently gloves were used because we have found no prints. A few of the women must have put up a good fight. We have been able to lift DNA samples from under their fingernails."

"No match in the DNA database though. That is about all we have at this point. We also do not have any solid suspects who match the collected evidence."

McCabe paged through the photographs taken at the crime scenes. One forensic report caught his eye. One of the victims appeared to have had a tooth physically removed.

"This could be something!" he said excitedly.

Montgomery leaned over his shoulder for a closer look. Her long dark hair fell across his shoulder.

"What have you got?"

"This girl had an extracted tooth."

"Jack, settle down, that is one tooth. Not her whole mouth like your case. It probably just fell out. Most of these girls are drug addicts too."

"Maybe nothing, just like the bones. I am heading over to look at x-rays of Denise Williams leg fracture this afternoon. I have a bone to pick with her doctor, so to speak. Want to join me?"

His dry humor amused her.

"Let's just keep it dinner tonight. You can tell me what you found out. If it is something, maybe we will be seeing a lot more of each other in the future."

"I like that Shelly. Especially that part about a lot more. See you tonight at the hotel restaurant."

"I have appointed one of my forensic doctors to examine the negatives."

McCabe left her office and drove to the hospital that worked on Denise Williams ten years ago. He was joined by Doctor Frank Benson, a top notch forensic investigator from Shelly's unit.

The x-rays were reviewed on a light screen. McCabe pulled his forensic team's x-rays of the partial torso and lower left leg. There were two distinct metal pins in both negatives.

Benson stood up for a closer examination. "Look at that," he said excitedly. "Both legs have pins in the exact locations."

"What does that mean?"

"It means it could be her. Lots of breaks get pinned in similar spots. What makes this interesting is that the top pin on both pictures is sticking out about a quarter inch. Not the best work by the surgeon. Normally they are flush with the bone. This makes me think it could definitely be a potential match."

"Wow. What is the next step to be sure it's her leg?"

Benson looked at the slide with his face as close as he could get to the picture.

"We need to blow this picture up in the lab. Usually we can match up a scratch or a break line. This looks really promising with the naked eye right now. A blow up will be conclusive proof it belongs to her."

"How long will it take you?"

"Probably by this afternoon if we process it right away."

McCabe drove him back to his office to begin work on the negative blow up.

In the lab, Benson placed the negatives in a machine which digitized the negatives. Then he loaded the digitized images into a computer and put them side by side on a large computer monitor.

With his mouse and specialized software he zoomed in on the steel medical pins. The first one had several distinct scratches on top where the screws had been tightened with instruments. Next the bone from McCabe's investigation was pulled up and zoomed. They looked exactly the same to the human eye.

Benson clicked the mouse on the compare button.

"Now let's see what the software thinks of these pictures. It scans for identical marks. If it gets ninety percent it marks it as a conclusive match."

"What about the other ten percent?" asked McCabe.

"The probability is ninety percent they are a match. Higher if the program comes back with a higher number. Most old bones we find always have some other marks on them. But scratches in medical screws almost always look the same."

The computer finished processing the pictures and the screen flashed "Match of 94 %."

"There you go. Your victim came from San Antonio. Or she at least lived and worked here for awhile."

McCabe happily thanked him. "I owe you one buddy. Lunch is on me when we have time. Not sure when that will be now with this new information. How about after we wrap this case up?"

Benson stopped him. "Sounds good to me, one more thing you should be aware of. See these little scratches sideways across the bone on the photo?"

McCabe nodded as he looked at the picture.

"That usually indicates the flesh was stripped from the bone with a tool, like a knife for example. If an anthropologist found scratches like this on a set of old bones, he would say it is indicative of cannibalism."

McCabe raised an eyebrow and thanked him again. "You do good work Benson. My forensic guys never told me that. Thanks."

Benson smiled. "Not every agency has this program yet. The software was just released as the latest and greatest forensic technology available."

McCabe patted him on the shoulder and left his lab. "I definitely owe you lunch, beers, whatever you want. This is big. This is huge. Nice work Benson."

He returned to his hotel and prepared for his dinner date with Shelly Montgomery. This is just great he thought to himself. He had an actual hard evidence lead and now a beautiful woman to work with. He just hoped she could put him on to more information to tie it together. He waited for Shelly in the hotel lobby.

She walked into the building and looked stunning wearing high heels and a tight white knit dress covering her well conditioned body. Her dark black hair fell across the white shoulders of her dress, contrasting nicely. She was an awesome sight.

"Hello gorgeous. You look dressed to kill."

"That's a joke. You know, we're serial murder investigators. Dressed to kill – get it? Bumbling, he tried to explain his logic. Anyway, you look great."

"That's my Jack. I missed that quick wit when our class went home," she said sarcastically. "I hoped we would see each other again."

"Actually, I did too. I thought about you a lot. I even picked up the phone once but chickened out."

"You were afraid of little old me? I didn't think I was that scary."

"Well, no. You're not scary. I didn't mean it like that exactly. It's just the way we left it in Denver. Sometimes it is better to just stay a memory. But right now I am really glad it is not just a memory."

They entered the restaurant and sat at a table overlooking the San Antonio River Walk. Small twinkle lights in the trees illuminated the meandering river.

"So, what did you find out this afternoon? I am extremely curious."

"We got a match on Benson's program. Ninety four percent match."

Her eyes opened wide. "You are kidding me!"

McCabe laughed and shook his head no.

"No, I am not. Honest to God truth. My victim was from San Antonio."

Montgomery took a sip of her wine. "Now if we could tie the cases together and find the killer, we would both be heroes."

McCabe agreed and pressed on. "Did you bring anyone in or have any leads on potential suspects?"

"Our search for the River Walk killer was primarily around local low life who hung out where these girls worked. Our prime suspect was a tour boat operator who liked the working girls who hung around his boat. It was just down the walk from Pedro's, a popular night club. He was a known customer of one of the victims we found."

She sipped her wine and continued briefing him on the River Walk case.

"We even did blood and tissue samples on her and matched them against his. We arrested him on suspicion of murder. She was last seen alive with him by one of her friends. He had no decent alibi so we arrested him. We thought he was involved because of prior john arrests and he beat up a hooker once. He hates these women but he continues to do business with them. The potential was there but we couldn't prove anything so we had to let him go."

"Who is this guy? Did you do a background check?"

"Yes we did and it was very interesting. His name is Kyle Standish. He was a military Special Forces candidate before a dishonorable discharge from Fort Collins, Oregon. He had survival training and almost finished the program with honors."

McCabe looked at her quizzically, "What is that supposed to mean?"

"They told us he displayed a tendency to be violent and cruel. They were preparing to give him a dishonorable discharge. He was convicted for dragging his girlfriend's dog behind his truck for spite after a breakup. Just what the military wants to see in a top notch candidate. He had a temper totally out of control."

"Sounds like a real asshole. So what happened to him?"

"Eventually he teamed up with another crazy buddy and crossed the military line before getting kicked out. They kidnapped and held their commanding officer hostage and nearly killed him. He was beaten very badly before a military Special Forces team rescued him and captured both of them."

"What did they give them?"

"They both did fifteen years hard time in military prison. They were trying to hold the military hostage for a weapons drop of serious proportions in the bush country of Washington state. They ordered five hundred M1's, grenade launchers, and a bunch of other weapons to be air dropped over a remote spot in the Cascade mountain range. If the military didn't comply, they were going to kill the commanding officer."

McCabe responded. "They sound like pretty serious guys and very stupid trying to take on the US military."

"Seems they were wrapped up in a since disbanded religious cult. They were trying to set up a well armed colony of survivalists, independent of the laws of the US Constitution. They actually wanted to hold a mountain top in the Cascades and secede from the Union. I think the military was bummed out because they caught them too soon. They wanted to put the whole bunch of them away. They viewed them as a domestic threat. They only got the two of them on kidnapping charges. Remember, this all happened before the days of the nine-eleven terrorism."

Shelly took a sip of her wine and continued.

"They both did only fifteen years for the crime with top notch lawyers defending them. Apparently, Kyle Standish has a father who was well connected with the military in arms development. He was the president of a company that manufactured high tech timer devices the military used for clocking navigational equipment. Anyhow, they could have both gotten life, but a plea agreement got them fifteen years without parole since no one was killed before it came to an end."

McCabe listened intently as she told the story.

"Just because of the nature of the crime, I think the prosecutors wanted to keep them locked up for good. The military does not usually mess around with mutiny and kidnapping of a superior officer. In this case, they bargained and made a slight exception. The men were only nineteen at the time and not in a combat situation. I guess that is how they justified it. Off the record, the word was a multi million dollar signed contract on equipment they valued highly at the time had something to do with it."

McCabe sat back in his chair adding up the prison sentence. "So they both got out of prison at about thirty four years old?"

"Yes, supposedly rehabilitated, but I was not convinced when I started investigating our suspect. If anything, I would say he is as crazy as he ever was. He had a history of violence in prison but always claimed he was attacked. He even killed an inmate in a fight once but didn't get any extra years. They called it self defense. Daddy got him off again."

"What happened to his partner in crime?"

Montgomery shrugged her shoulders. "Our suspect placed him in northern Idaho. He said he was going to go back and live off the land. We briefly tried to contact him but we could never track him down. We tried contacting his parents but they died in a plane crash. Finally, a neighbor in the town of Boise claimed he said he was moving to the Midwest. He didn't know where though."

"That's a lot of time to do together and not stay in touch. Then again, maybe not if it was too much time. Did he act like they were friends in prison?"

Montgomery responded. "Not really, over the years they blamed each other for their predicament behind bars. Seems they went their separate ways after many prison fights and a large degree of hatred for each other. The only thing our man would say is that he hopes the big son of a bitch is dead. He acted like he was afraid of him."

McCabe's attention perked up from the last statement. "The big son of a bitch, that's interesting."

"The thumb print I lifted off the boat was abnormally large. I remember first thinking it must be a side palm print, until I looked at it closer. It's probably nothing but you never know. If he was in prison they will have prints on him. What is his name?"

"Tom Jepson. Our suspect said he went by the nickname, "The Griffin" in prison. It's a mythical monster with the body and hind legs of a lion, and the head and the wings of an eagle. Jepson was very crazy and officially referred to himself as Prometheus the Griffin. He read a lot of Greek mythology in prison and thought he was one of them. According to Greek mythology, Prometheus was a Titan who stole fire from heaven for the benefit of mankind. For his punishment, Zeus chains him to a rock where a vulture or eagle comes each day to eat his liver which grows back each night."

She continued explaining what the Kyle Standish had told her.

"The other prisoners were totally terrified of this guy who called himself Prometheus the Griffin. One guy in prison told us he was the craziest guy in the joint. Jepson threatened he would eat the man's liver if he didn't obey him. He wanted to extort money from his family on the outside. And he was physically intimidating. The inmate got himself put in segregation on purpose, just to get away from Jepson. He is about six foot six and around three hundred pounds of pure muscle, I was told. The inmate felt he would kill him for sure if he didn't agree to his demands."

Montgomery paused, "So much for my case, now tell me about yours."

McCabe elaborated on his case and the gory details of torsos and body parts floating up all over the lake. He started to tell about the skeleton and the Caldwell brothers but stopped.

"I don't want to make you sick."

The conversation turned to their times together in evidence class. They shared some lighter moments and the nice evenings they had all week long.

"We were lucky to even get to class a few of those mornings," said Montgomery.

"I would call in sick with you every chance I could Shelly."

As the evening wound down, they returned to McCabe's room for a cocktail. The conversation turned back to work.

"One other thing I just thought of that bothers me. It's that skeleton story you started to tell me about. We had a case down here of a rural family out in the hillsides. It was a gory mess in a little run down shack in the foothill country. Parts of the bodies had been stripped of flesh. They convicted the husband but he claimed he didn't do it. He said it was an intruder in the night. He described the attacker as some big guy with a beard who knocked him out and took his family. The jury said otherwise and convicted him. Authorities found three bodies scattered along the hillside. Two of them were young kids. They were stripped of flesh by the buzzards and such. Pretty gross I heard."

"Is the husband still in jail?"

"He has been in there for about five years now. He got life without parole. To this day he still claims he had nothing to do with it."

"Well, hopefully they didn't lock up the wrong guy. This case will still be here tomorrow. Remember, all work and no play makes Jack a dull boy. If the prints check out we will talk to some of these guys tomorrow."

McCabe reached over and turned out the light on the nightstand.

Their bodies merged together as the moonlight softly illuminated the hotel room.

8

McCabe drove her home in the morning and then called back to his home office.

"Captain Becker. What's up McCabe?"

"Hey Cap. Just wondering if that thumb print scan came back yet?"

"I will check and call you back in about twenty minutes."

McCabe watched Montgomery climb the steps to her condo and go inside. A beautiful sight he thought as he started his car. This business trip was already turning out to be a great one.

His cell phone rang as he pulled up to the Federal Building. It was Captain Becker.

"This is Jack, what do you have Cap?"

"You are not going to believe this Jack. We got a match. It belongs to an ex-con named Tom Jepson."

"You got to be kidding me!" exclaimed McCabe.

"He did hard time for a military crime about twenty years ago."

McCabe interrupted him. "I know about him already. The trail is heating up. I need to find out more about this guy. Can you email me the file they provided on him? It might have some additional information I have not already heard."

"Sure, but how do you know about him already?"

"Let's just say I work hard getting inside to obtain information. It is a tough job but someone has to do it. By the way, the femur bone was a match too."

Captain Becker shook his head. "I can only imagine McCabe. Okay, time to profile this guy and nail him."

The file showed Jepson to be a less than model inmate and a big man indeed. He was six foot six and three hundred and twenty five pounds according to the prison data. And he carried a reputation which was feared by his fellow inmates, earning him the name Griffin.

He continued to study the email in Shelly Montgomery's office, waiting for her to arrive. She walked in about 9:00 AM, wearing blue jeans and a casual black vest.

"You're late agent Montgomery. Late night last night?" he quipped, chuckling.

"Very funny, Jack."

"The print came back this morning. It is Tom Jepson's thumb."

"What!" she exclaimed.

"That's right. I have his file right here and have been studying it all morning."

"Okay, so that means our primary suspect in River Walk and your primary suspect for the Tanner's Lake murders did time together. What does that mean?"

"I am not sure yet, but I intend to find out. For starters, I would like to bring your suspect back in for more questioning."

"We can do that, but we have to be careful. Standish will threaten harassment as we already had him in and let him go."

"Let him threaten. This is new hard evidence on a different case placing his former partner in crime at the actual scene. If he doesn't cooperate, I will threaten him with being an accessory on the Tanner's Lake murders."

Shelly smiled at him. "Let's go get him partner. I want to see if I like working with you as much as I like sleeping with you."

She grabbed her chrome .45 caliber two shot derringer and stuck it in her vest pocket.

"You are carrying enough for both of us. This should do for this trip". She actually had a .45 automatic government issue in her purse as well.

McCabe put on his coat and they left for the River Walk.

Tourists lined the River Walk near the tour boats. The boats took large groups of tourists down the river winding through downtown San Antonio.

"That looks like fun," said McCabe.

As they neared the last of the tourist boats they bordered the night club district. Some of the working girls were standing around Pedro's near Standish's boat.

Montgomery pointed him out from a distance.

"That's Standish right over there on the last boat."

McCabe walked up to him first with Shelly standing back observing in case he ran.

"Nice boat." He flashed his FBI credentials. "I need to talk to you about your old buddy Tom Jepson."

The man immediately balked and told him to buzz off.

"I already talked to the fed's about him and I'm done talking with you. Get off my boat."

McCabe winced. "I'm afraid it's not that easy pal. This is a different case I am working on. You can either come with me down to our office or I will arrest you right now."

The man shook his head and suddenly bolted in Shelly's direction. She popped out from around a corner just as he was approaching with the .45 automatic from her purse drawn.

Pointing it directly at his head from ten feet away, she ordered him to lie flat. By the time McCabe got there in pursuit she already had him cuffed.

"Nice gun, I thought you carried a derringer?" he commented as he helped get Standish to his feet. For a small petite woman he had heard Shelly could be pretty tough. It didn't hurt that she was a black belt in karate either. They ordered a squad to pick up Standish and take him downtown for them.

"I thought you might try to take him out with a karate move or something," quipped a smiling McCabe.

"That's the movies Jack. That's why I carry a gun. So I don't have to get physical."

McCabe grinned. "Oh yeah, I understand completely. You wouldn't want to get physical or anything like that. Who ever said mixing business and pleasure was a bad idea anyway?"

"I think you said that Jack. About two years ago to me after our class one night."

"Oh. Okay… well maybe I was wrong about that."

"Maybe you were right about that Jack. Especially if you don't shut up and get down to business. You should have caught that guy before he ever got to me."

"Okay. Okay. Maybe you're right. I didn't think he would just run like that though. It won't happen again."

"Don't worry about it. Let's go see what he has to say."

Downtown they had Mr. Standish waiting for them in an interrogation room with two-way glass.

Shelly watched from the outside as McCabe started to interrogate him.

"Tell me about your prison buddy Tom Jepson."

Standish was a good sized man standing about six feet and approximately forty years old.

"He's an asshole. What else do you need to know about him?"

"That's a start. When did you see him last?

"I don't have to talk to you."

"No you don't. Do you like prison?"

"What is that supposed to mean?"

"It means… I could send you back to prison for withholding information on a murder case we believe Tom Jepson is involved in."

"Who did he kill this time?"

McCabe bent over the table and repeated him.

"You said this time. Were there more killings?"

Standish squirmed in his chair. "I don't know."

"Well why did you say that?"

"I don't know. I want to see a lawyer."

"You already waived your right to counsel when they booked you. You were offered a phone call and refused. You get one call a day. Better call him tomorrow."

"That's a shitty deal."

"Yeah, a lot of things in life are a shitty deal. Like for example, if you got locked up for a long time because of something Jepson did. I thought you said he was an asshole. Why are you protecting him?"

"I'm not protecting him. He is nuts big time. The last time I saw him he said he was killing for fun. He said sometimes he was a cannibal and got power from human flesh. He was totally crazy and I'm afraid of him."

"When did you see him?"

"He was in San Antonio about a year ago."

"Did he stay at your place?"

"No."

"You and him both liked the hookers didn't you?"

"What makes you think that?"

"We know he stayed at your place. We have evidence."

"Like what? He had a shack in the foot hills 20 miles out of town."

"Can you take us there?"

"No. I don't know where it is."

"I think you do. Is that where you took the girls?"

He smiled at McCabe. "You will have to find him and ask him."

"You like the girls all dressed up in nice clothes don't you? Did you dress them up at his place?"

"Is that Jepson's DNA inside all the dead girls?"

"You don't really like them for sex do you? You just like to dress them up."

"I am not talking anymore without an attorney."

"Daddy is pretty good at finding you attorneys isn't he?"

He became extremely agitated with the last comment. "Leave my father out of this!"

"Why should I? Maybe your father would be interested to know you like to dress up dead hookers like they were Barbie dolls. Did you play with Barbie dolls as a kid? I'm going to talk to him and tell him everything."

Standish violently lunged at McCabe in anger. A large deputy in the room sat him back down. Then he began to cry and started to break.

"He made me dress them up after he raped and killed them. Then he told me to get rid of them or he would sodomize me and eat my flesh in front of me while I was still alive. I was afraid of what he would do to me."

"I bet you liked dressing the girls up though didn't you? That's why you got the hookers for him wasn't it?"

He grew suddenly calm in an instant.

"Yes. I didn't kill them though."

"Why should I believe that? You have killed in the past."

"I killed an inmate in prison to survive."

"Okay. But you took them to his place so he could rape them."

"Yes."

"Anything else you want to tell me? The more you tell the easier it will be on you. You kidnapped those girls when you took them to his place in the hills."

"The first one I thought we would just go out there for some fun. I would dress her up like a model and he would have sex with her. Then I would take her home. But he killed her when he was through. After he killed her he made me bring him more girls."

"Where is Jepson now?"

"I don't know. He said he was heading north to start another survivalist group. He was going to live off the land somewhere in the woods. He liked the woods and the animals. He talked about them all the time. He left with one of the girls I got for him."

"Who was that?"

"Denise Williams. He was keeping her as his sex slave."

McCabe looked out the window at Shelly Montgomery. It had come full circle. In a thirty minute interrogation he had cracked the case wide open. They now knew who they were looking for. The cases were linked.

"We will talk again this afternoon. Maybe you will remember more." McCabe walked out of the interrogation room and looked at Montgomery.

"Well partner, looks like we will be working together for sure now. You are going to love the north woods."

Montgomery sat on the edge of her desk stunned but in awe of how he handled the interrogation and got Standish to confess.

"What was that about we have evidence he stayed at your place?"

"I lied. I must have been thinking about another case. Just an honest mistake I guess. I was confused."

McCabe smiled knowingly and put his arm around her.

"Hopefully they will not turn that into a coerced confession somehow," she replied.

"I don't think so. Now all we have to do is find the mountain shack and get hard evidence. Then you have the number two man and your prime suspect.

You were right on, that he was involved. He just wasn't the one having sex with them and killing them. When we capture Mr. Jepson, his DNA will match the samples you took from the River Walk victims. Military prison did not sample him or we could check right now."

"You make it all seem so easy Jack."

"Not at all Shelly, all we know is who this guy is now. The problem is we don't know where he is. I have a pretty good idea of where to start looking though."

Shelly looked at him in awe. "Do you always ride into town like John Wayne and save the day?" she asked.

He was modest.

"I got lucky. If it wasn't that stuff about his dad he probably never would have cracked. I took a long shot from some information I read on his psychological report this morning."

He picked up the report and glanced at it again.

"The report said his father once caught him playing with dolls as a young boy and beat him for it. From a psychological perspective he was really messed up. His father wanted him to be a macho athlete which he never lived up to. I just played on his feminine side. I was hoping he would be sensitive to us talking to him about dolls. Then that Barbie stuff, I just made it up from what you had told me about the case, how the victims were dressed up in nice clothes. He obviously got upset about that."

Montgomery smiled across the table. "You certainly have a way with words Jack. I noticed that the first night you tried to seduce me."

McCabe opened the office door and suggested they break for lunch. "Let's see what Standish has to say in the afternoon session. Then I will be heading back to Minnesota and Tanner's Lake. Do you want to come with me?"

Montgomery straightened up and looked him directly in the eye.

"I most certainly do. This is my case, too. I've spent a lot of time involved looking for both of these guys. Now that we have something big going, I definitely want to be a part of it. Besides, Jepson sounds dangerous. You might need the help from what I saw this morning bringing in Kyle Standish."

McCabe laughed. "No problem. Like I said before, whoever said you can't mix business and pleasure?"

"That was you Jack."

When they returned from lunch, Mr. Standish was once again in the interrogation room.

McCabe entered the room. "Did you get some lunch?"

"What do you care?"

"Just wondering, you probably like prison food I bet."

"No. It's slop."

"What else can you tell me about Jepson?"

"What is there to know?"

Standish paused for a moment.

"He is a crazy cannibal who likes the woods and animals. He claims he can talk to animals and they talk back to him."

"Like what kind of animals?"

"Mostly birds. He liked birds. He used to do hunting by falconry. He knows how to train them."

"Anything else you can think of?"

"He likes most animals and tried to tame them when we were in Oregon as young men. He had a mean dog he used to like. He would try to train it as a watch dog for our camp."

"What else does he know about living in the bush country?"

"Everything there is to know. He is an expert hunter, fisherman woodsman and basically a very capable survivalist. He can live off most anything."

"Really, like how do you mean?"

"You know those survivalist TV shows where guys eat worms to stay alive?

"Yeah, like that?"

"He would eat a bucket of worms and wash it down with human blood and think he just had a five course meal. He would enjoy it."

"Is he a cannibal?"

"Yes."

"How do you know? None of the girl's bodies were devoured."

"Not the girls. He only did it when he needed food in the bush. I saw him do it to a guy who died of fever in our group in Washington."

"He told me he did it once here too. He told me he was getting used to it and said he was developing a taste for it."

"Was it that foot hills case with the family that had their flesh stripped?"

"Yes. He told me he lived off their flesh for three weeks hiding in the foot hills after the murders."

"Did he say anything else about it?"

"No. Nothing else comes to mind."

"Alright Kyle, we will talk again."

"Can I go back to my boat now?"

"I'm afraid not Kyle. You are going to be booked as an accomplice to the River Walk murders."

McCabe left the room as another FBI agent entered and proceeded to read a protesting Kyle Standish his rights. Shelly approached him as he came out and spoke.

"We probably have had an innocent man in jail for five years for the murder of his family. We have to get this new information to the court system right now."

McCabe nodded. "When we catch Jepson, hopefully he will admit it."

McCabe sat down at Shelly's desk, spent from the intense questioning. His thoughts turned to Minnesota and a cannibal roaming the woods somewhere.

The woods of northern Minnesota were so thick you could barely walk through them in the summer time. Hot nights with usually high humidity made everything grow like weeds. The woods became as thick as a jungle with green leafed plants and trees growing profusely.

Add lots of trees on the ground from a recent blow down, vicious insects, and the sheer size of the forest itself made it a great place to hide out. Jepson would be tough to find.

"I will be leaving in the morning," said McCabe.

Shelly looked at him. "I have already made accommodations near the Minneapolis airport. I have us booked for an 11:00AM flight."

"Separate rooms I hope."

"Of course, I wouldn't want to start any rumors about us."

McCabe stood up and looked at the summer outfit Shelly was wearing.

"You best pack a bunch of casual clothes. Northern Minnesota is nothing like south Texas. Bring lots of blue jeans, sweatshirts, T-shirts, coats, you name it."

"The summer weather can range from one hundred degree highs to thirty degree lows and everything in between. It can be hotter than blazes and the next thing you know, a storm rolls in with a cold rain and it's suddenly forty five degrees on a windy lake."

Montgomery looked at him sternly. "Don't worry. I will be able to handle it. I thrive on adverse conditions."

"We'll see. I am just warning you. We can buy some things up there more suited for the climate. The weather can kill you in that land if you are not ready for it."

McCabe started walking out of her office and turned at the door.

"After packing do you want to show me the night life of San Antonio? I would love one of those tour boat rides down the river at night."

"No problem Jack. I will see you about 8pm at my place."

McCabe grinned. "Okay then. It's a date."

He started through the door.

"Hey Jack. Thanks for everything today. Nice job."

He stopped and smiled. "Thank you Miss Montgomery. I couldn't have done it without you."

McCabe exited the room and headed back to his hotel. This is good he thought. I always wanted to work as a team with a sharp female agent. And Shelly was much more than just a working partner. He had definite feelings for her.

He hoped she could adapt to the new environment she was about to experience. He had no doubt Jepson was an extremely dangerous man. He would have to hunt him in his own territory which made him even more deadly.

In some ways he wished he could finish this case alone. It was going to take some serious tracking in the northern forest to catch this guy. Something more suited for a local deer hunter like himself, not a south Texas girl with an understanding of the woods as a big grove of trees in a river ravine. He hoped she would not be a burden in the *big* woods of the north.

9

The young hawks had been taken from their nests one year ago. The big man moved around the shack talking to the bird on his arm. He picked a mouse from a trap in the filthy cabin and held it up in front of the bird of prey.

"Maybe you do not like small rodents anymore?"

"Maybe you only want bigger animals like our friends from the lake? We will go to school now my feathered friend."

He released the tethered bird from his arm and let it fly up. Placing the dead mouse on his shoulder he pointed his big hand swiftly down in a swooping motion.

The bird responded to his hand signal from high above and swooped in at high speed, snatching the mouse from his shoulder. The Griffin was pleased. He believed he was a mythical creature and at one with birds.

His self given name was Prometheus based on Greek mythology. Prometheus was a Titan who stole fire from heaven for the benefit of mankind. For his punishment from Zeus, he was chained to a rock where an eagle comes each day to eat his liver, which grows back each night. He knew Greek mythology well and loved to think of the birds. He wondered about the legend of the man who made wings that melted when he flew too close to the sun. He often wished he could fly like his birds.

He chose Prometheus as he believed his body renewed itself when injured. Like Prometheus, someday he would feed his liver to the eagle. The big bald eagle always stayed within close proximity of Prometheus the Griffin. He was very proud of his eagle.

As the Griffin, he could always provide food for the eagle. The Griffin was an efficient hunter. He played the same bird game as with the hawks, only with larger animals. Prometheus would place a dead rabbit or fish on his shoulder. With his right hand, he would circle his arm up and then point it swiftly down. Since an eaglet, the now adult bird understood the feeding command. The eagle swooped in and grabbed the dead rabbit from his shoulder with amazing speed and accuracy.

“Someday this will be my liver,” he shouted as the bird flew off with the dead rabbit.

He rarely had to lure the eagle back with bait anymore. It would perch on top of a high tree and watch the Griffin’s daily routine, hoping for more food.

Much of the day involved checking the spiked animal pits. As the big man moved up the trail leading to his shack he suddenly stopped. Evergreen boughs covered the forest floor. He carefully walked around as did his wolf dog trailing behind him. Farther up the trail they came to an area with boughs around the edge and an apparent hole at one end. The Griffin smiled and spoke to his dog.

“Let us see what we have for supper tonight.”

Removing the pine boughs, it revealed a six foot deep hole with a deer impaled on sharp wooden stakes at the bottom. Still alive, the animal kicked and struggled to get out to no avail. The buck deer was severely injured and slowly dying.

The Griffin looked down at the struggling animal and spoke.

"How do you want to die my four legged friend?"

"I could let Lobo run you down and kill you with his sharp fangs. Or, do you prefer the claws of steel from Prometheus the Griffin?"

He thought for a moment as if listening for a response. Then he made the decision. He reached down and grabbed the struggling buck's antlers and pulled the deer partially up with incredible strength.

Holding it with one hand he pulled a large knife from a sheath strapped to his thigh and sliced the animal's throat in one fluid motion. He dragged the deer head over the edge of the pit and let his dog clamp on to the bleeding throat.

The animal thrashed momentarily as he held it suspended from the antlers over the edge. As he pulled the dead deer up the rest of the way, he slapped the snarling dog's head from the deer's throat.

"Enough!" he bellowed.

The dog released the deer's throat and backed off from the large man as if fearful to not obey.

"You always obey the Griffin or you will wind up for supper like the deer."

He spoke softly now to the dog. "You will get your fill soon. You can bring the head back to camp for me."

With that he continued slicing the deer's throat, decapitating the head and throwing it to the dog. He proceeded to gut the deer pulling out the heart. He took a bite of the organ as if it were an apple and chewed the muscle speaking to his dog. Blood ran down the Griffin's beard and dripped to the ground.

"Yes, we will feed well tonight. Tonight we will even make fire from the heavens and eat cooked flesh. The smoke of the tourist camp fires will mask our hideout. We will be campers just like all the others tonight."

Most of the year, he ate meat raw to keep people from finding him. He was aware of the forest service and how they looked for smoke in remote areas. He remembered his punishment from Zeus for fire. His liver would grow back, he thought. He would have roasted deer flesh tonight.

He quartered the deer and placed it in a duffel bag to obscure it from view. He walked through the woods dragging his canoe and duffel to the lake's edge. He threw the canvas bag into the canoe and pushed off. His dog laid down on the duffel bag. His birds followed him from the air.

He spoke to his dog. "We will eat and sleep at the cave. It is better cover than the cabin."

As he paddled past the boat landing he saw an angler launching a boat.

"We must avoid the landing unless we need to hunt the flesh of the human. We will eat the hoofed animal of the forest tonight."

The angler waved as he paddled past, unaware of the monster inside the canoe. They are such easy prey thought the Griffin. Humans had provided his sustenance much of the winter.

The canoe moved slow along the shoreline of Rice Bay and disappeared in a small lily pad cove. He paddled to the end of the shallow cove behind a beaver house until he hit shore. He dragged the canoe up on shore and hid it back in the bulrushes lining the bank.

From there they made their way up a small path that looked like a deer trail. They began the steep climb up the hill. With the duffel slung over his shoulder, the big man carried the hind quarters of the deer with ease. His dog followed him into the tangled sumacs growing at the top of the hill.

This led to the cliff ledge below. Through the thick foliage, he could see patches of the blue water from the lake far below. He pushed the big rock from the opening and entered his lair. A fire pit with a roasting spit sat in the middle of the cave room. He moved two large poles of camouflaged burlap overhanging the cave opening from the cliff edge. It revealed a view of the bay below when removed. A small opening in the foliage about the size of a window allowed the sunshine to illuminate the inside of the cave. The rock floor had steel animal traps scattered about. Iron shackles were screwed into the cave wall giving it a dungeon like appearance.

He had a camouflaged military ammo box which he opened. He pulled a butane torch from the box and smiled at his dog.

"I am a woodsman and a hunter. I am also a scholar and a gentleman. I use some of man's best inventions. And fire which is my gift to mankind."

With that he clicked the butane fire starter and a flame jumped off the end. "Most do not know that this was a gift Prometheus brought from heaven."

He lit the pile of wood and opened the duffel bag, hanging the rear leg quarters from the cave wall. Ten inch steel pins embedded in the wall easily penetrated the rear leg tendons. He sawed off a large chunk of meat and laid it on the rocks by the fire to roast.

His dog looked at the meat on the ground and whined softly. The Griffin sawed another chunk and threw it to the begging animal.

"Watch the hill," he ordered, throwing the dog a bone.

The wolf dog trotted up the ledge with a bone in its mouth.

He speared a piece of meat with his long bowie knife and placed it on the metal spit. Looking down he saw the angler that had just launched his boat.

"You should not fish in Rice Bay my friend," he said, talking to himself. He moved a log onto the flames increasing the fire's intensity.

"The Indian man treats me well to scare you away. He trades me tobacco and alcohol and keeps my secret. He feeds me in the winter time. You should beware of the Griffin. So should the Indian. I could eat you both if you betray me."

He began to eat the barely cooked meat, ripping it from the bone with his strong jawbone. He thought about the Indian man.

He had not seen him for a long time. It had been since last winter. When he came to the lake from the south, the Indian man offered him shelter and refuge in exchange for the woman he kept.

The Indian told him of the legend and the curse. The Griffin felt it was his destiny to watch the bay and protect it. He gave the Indian man his money he had earned in prison from terrorizing the weak inmates. He had no use for US currency. He did not need it anymore.

The Indian told him if he watched the bay for white intruders the gods would be pleased. He felt it was his place in the universe to help fulfill the curse legacy and avenge the wrong doing of the white society. The Griffin felt sorry for the Indian people and hated the white civilized world for what they had done to them. He hated the US Government and how it pushed people off their lands. If he protected the bay from the intruders, maybe Zeus would forgive him.

He thought about the wonderful stories he learned as an inmate reading Greek Mythology in the prison library. Now he was a living legend of god like proportions. He was Prometheus, a Titan legend. He was a giant among mortal men and now his mission was to please Zeus.

By carrying out the Indian curse he could convince Zeus to free him from the rock and eagle. To forgive him for the fire he had given man. To let him live in peace with the gods.

The Griffin tore more meat from bone. He would do anything to be free from the wrath of the gods. He roasted the purple deer liver. He wondered if it grew back like his.

The Griffin's mind was twisted from reality. He lived like a cave man awaiting another day and another meal. But he was more resourceful than the cave man. He could eat and enjoy human flesh as well. This was because he ruled above man and had spoken with the gods.

A hawk flew in and perched on a tree branch close to the cave opening. He spoke to the bird.

"Tonight we will watch the bay. If they fish at night they will be sorry. They will meet the Griffin."

The big man looked down on the boat drift fishing the bay and began to softly chuckle. His thoughts tickled him and he erupted into the uproarious bellowing laugh of a crazed lunatic.

He pulled a whisky bottle from one of the metal canisters and took a long pull. After eating his fill of venison, the Griffin laid down on the pine bough bed lining the cave floor. As he drifted to sleep he thought about the upcoming night.

I must be rested, he thought, to protect the bay from intruders. He pondered the fact that Zeus would be pleased with his efforts. Someday he would be free from the wrath of the gods.

10

As the plane made its approach on the runway, McCabe reached over and held Shelly's hand. It was always a good feeling to hear the wheels touch down and feel the plane slow to a stop. They had just landed at Minneapolis International Airport on a beautiful spring day.

"I should take you around and show you the sights," said McCabe. "Kind of return the favor for the San Antonio tour."

"That would be nice but we need to get down to business finding this guy before he kills again."

McCabe agreed. "You are absolutely right that we need to stay focused on this case. But when it is over you promise me a week to display my tour guide skills".

Shelly Montgomery sensed her strong attraction to McCabe and was glad to be with him in Minneapolis. She hoped things would continue after the case ended.

McCabe's vehicle was still parked at the airport so they retrieved his truck for transportation. After a short drive they arrived at the hotel.

"Well here we are at another hotel room," said McCabe.

"We could head up to Tanner's Lake today if we want to. How does a romantic cabin with a fireplace on a lake sound?"

Shelly liked the idea very much. "That would be absolutely fabulous. We can stay here when you show me the Twin Cities before I go back to San Antonio. I'm excited to see this rugged landscape you talk about from a rustic little cabin."

"Okay then, I must say I like spontaneity in my life. It keeps one feeling young."

They threw their luggage back in the truck and headed out on the highway. "It is about a three hour drive to Tanner's Lake from here," said McCabe.

As the truck cruised down the interstate, talk turned to capturing Tom Jepson. Shelly was digging through her bag looking over the things she had packed.

She began to pull them out showing McCabe.

"Standard issue bullet proof vest, I thought it might come in handy."

"No doubt about that. And it will help keep you warm too."

"You are obsessed about the northern cold. It is seventy degrees out today Jack. It's perfect weather."

"It is also 1:00PM and May 21st in Minnesota."

"Yeah, Memorial weekend and full blown summer coming up," she responded.

"Okay, what else do you have along?" asked Jack.

She pulled out her .45 caliber automatic pistol. Next she pulled out the two shot chrome derringer with a special holster designed for mounting on her lower calf ankle area.

"It is a nice backup if you are in a jam. It saved my life once. I never go anywhere without it," she smiled.

"Just like a credit card I guess," he joked.

Next she pulled out a knife. A six inch stiletto she flicked open in an instant. "It is sharpened on both sides. I have it filed down like a razor," she said. "Better if you have to slash."

"Those are illegal in the States you know."

"Not for FBI agents. My uncle in Mexico gave it to me as a present once for Christmas. He thought it might come in handy on my new job."

"It's nice to get to know about your family. Maybe I can meet your parents sometime. What did they give you? An AK47 for traveling in the desert?" he said a bit sarcastically.

"Actually no, but they did give me this."

She pulled a sharp six pointed metal star out of a small black carrying case with a belt loop used for concealment on the small of your back.

"This is a throwing star. They gave it to me when I got my black belt at age nineteen. You throw it overhand like a baseball and it sticks every time as one point always hits."

"Nice." McCabe shook his head chuckling.

"Once again they thought it would help protect me. I explained to them that karate was about self defense and not using your skills to hurt people. I assured them I didn't need it but they insisted. I think it was a little girl thing leaving the nest for a dangerous job in the big city. You know, give her a bunch of tools of the trade to protect her. At least that's what they were thinking."

"Once again illegal in most states," said McCabe.

"Once again, not if you are an FBI agent," she responded.

McCabe looked at her and laughed out loud.

"You are kidding me right? Is this a good thing or a bad thing? It appears I am involved with a woman of lethal capabilities."

She looked at him seductively. "That would be a good thing as I am your partner Jack. I might have to save your life or you mine. We can have no secrets at this point."

"Just don't be showing that stuff off to these country cops we will be meeting tomorrow. They probably won't understand."

Montgomery nodded her head. “No problem Jack. I don’t want to upset the Mayberry police. Does Barney Fife work there?”

“Good one. These guys are actually pretty sharp though. And we need their help.”

Shelly took on a more serious tone. “How hard do you *really* think this guy will be to catch? I mean, you were raised in these parts. Do you think he is dangerous to the point we need to be worried now that we have identified him?”

McCabe looked at her deadly serious. “I think it is going to be extremely dangerous from what I know about this guy so far. It is not like we are going to just walk up to his house and arrest him.”

“Where do you think his house is?” replied Montgomery.

McCabe thought a moment. “I think he could be on the Indian reservation somewhere on the north end of the lake. No reason really, other than I got attacked by birds there about two weeks ago while fishing.”

“Is that cut on your arm from that?” she asked.

“Yes, it is. It was really weird. An eagle and a hawk were dive bombing me on the lake. The locals think it was because I had a fish in the bottom of the boat that they wanted. I am not so sure now from what Standish said. I think this guy may have already drawn first blood on me.”

Shelly took a closer look at his forearm on the steering wheel.

“I have never heard of anything like that before. I mean, everybody has had the dive bombing song bird when you come near the nest. Isn’t it pretty weird to get attacked by birds of prey?”

McCabe nodded in agreement. “For sure, and now I learn about this ex-convict’s prison reputation. He was like the Bird Man of Alcatraz or something. He specialized in training birds of prey. They call them hawkers, those guys who hunt with falcons and hawks. Maybe he has taken his training a step further somehow.”

“You really think so?”

McCabe shook his head. “I don’t know. I really couldn’t say if it is possible to train birds to attack humans. If anyone could do it, this guy would be the type that might have the skill to pull it off. Probably no one has ever really tried to get birds to dive bomb humans.”

McCabe went on. “There is this weird Indian legend thing going on up there too. Something about a white man will protect Rice Bay from intruders for the Indian nation. Rice Bay is where I got attacked.”

Shelly pondered for a moment. “Interesting, maybe an Indian is paying him off or something.”

“I have considered that possibility. I went to the reservation and met a few of them. I heard an old man tell me about the legend.”

“Maybe it is the old man.”

“I don’t think so but you never know. We will be meeting some more Native Americans at Flanagan’s resort. They hang out at a bar there.”

“Okay, so I guess we hang out there with them? Do they know you are an FBI agent?”

“No, not as far as I know anyway. I never mentioned that I was an FBI agent to these guys. But others might know about me. I was asking a lot of questions farther up the lake at other resorts.”

“Did you get any leads?”

“Maybe one, a local resident on a snowmobile described a very big primitive looking dude pulling a toboggan across the ice one night last winter. I think he was dumping a body in the frozen lake through an ice house.”

“You are kind of losing a girl who grew up in south Texas her whole life. I have never been on a frozen lake before.”

McCabe explained. “They drive cars and have fires on the ice too. It gets four feet thick in the middle of winter. A lot of fishermen consider the frozen lake their home away from home. They put up small wooden ice shacks with heaters in them. Some people make them pretty nice and even sleep overnight in them. Others make bonfires on the ice and fish into the night around them to keep warm."

"That's amazing. Fire on the ice and it doesn't melt it?"

"It does, but not fast enough. Especially if you float the wood above the snow with some pine boughs. It gets cold up north in the winter."

"Okay, whatever, I will take your word for it. I will probably be gone before winter anyway," she responded.

"Hopefully we will catch him way before then."

McCabe put the truck on cruise control as they rolled north on interstate 35W.

"I certainly hope so but there are no guarantees in this business. He could up and leave anytime if he thinks we are on to him. An alert is now out that he is wanted in connection with murders in Texas and possibly Minnesota. I have already called my boss and informed him of the situation. He is taking the steps and getting Jepson on the FBI's most wanted list."

As they moved north the scenery began to change from farms to more woodland. The divided highway split apart as they coursed through the thick woods. As a car passed them Shelly read the license plate.

"The plate read Land of 10,000 Lakes. Are there really that many?"

"Actually, there are more than that I guess. I think they only count them if they are over ten acres or something like that."

They passed a lake along the highway as the car continued northbound.

"There's one right there," said McCabe.

"That is nothing compared to Tanner's Lake though. It's a huge lake. They say it's about nine hundred miles of shoreline all the way around it." Jack slowed down for a quick view of the small lake they were passing.

"Tanner's Lake also has literally hundreds of little bays and islands scattered all over it too. It would take a long time to search it all, and a lot of places to hide out if that was your mission in life."

"Maybe I will be here in the wintertime. I would love to try one of those snow machines," she replied.

The car came over the steep hill into the shipping town of Duluth. The high elevation showed the large expanse of blue water stretching across the horizon to be Lake Superior with the Saint Louis River entering the big lake from the south.

"Wow, that is a really pretty view," said Montgomery. The car wound down the big hill toward the lake.

"That is the biggest of the Great Lakes. To be exact, Lake Superior and the tourist town and shipping port of Duluth. It's the biggest freshwater lake in the world," he responded.

"How am I doing as your tourist guide?"

"Just fine Jack. I am impressed," she said looking out the window.

Bridges crisscrossed the big blue water bay as the car continued downward. Great Lakes ore boats and ocean going ships dotted the harbor. About another hour north of here and we will be at the town of Jackson. As they moved farther north they followed the rocky shore line of the big lake.

"This is really beautiful country," commented Montgomery.

McCabe pulled the car up to a specialty outfitters store. "We need to buy you some clothes. Come on."

She looked at him quizzically. "You don't like how I dress?"

McCabe laughed. "I do. You just need different stuff up in the lake country. Trust me. I need to make you blend in more with the locals and tourists. Think of it as your undercover outfit."

"Okay, let's go shopping Mr. McCabe."

Inside the store were canvas packs and warm outdoor clothing. There was a variety of merchandise for sale, mostly high end camping gear and clothing.

She tried on a down ski jacket and some wool leggings for the outside of her jeans. She topped it off with a pair of gloves and a small woolen cap. Hiking boots and a few more pairs of jeans and vests and she was ready to check out.

She looked great in her new apparel. She picked out a few souvenir T-shirts and sweatshirts as well for the changing weather.

McCabe watched her model the clothes from the changing room and approved.

"Awesome. You look right at home and should stay warm now. You can get a couple more shirts at Tanner's Lake. It is good to have a little bit of everything. You can dress in layers too if it gets really cold."

"I thought you were supposed to keep me warm." she joked.

"That is exactly what I am doing. You will thank me if we are out on the lake at night."

Back on the road the scenery continued to change as they moved farther north into the woods. Rugged granite rocky outcroppings bordered the roadside. The forest was mostly thick pine, aspen and maple trees.

"I have not seen a lake for awhile." said Montgomery.

McCabe responded, "They are out there. You just can't see them from the road. When you fly over this country you will be amazed at how much water there really is."

"Can we do that?" she asked.

"I intend to have a search and rescue plane fly us around Tanner's Lake. I want to see it from the air. It will give us a better idea of what we are looking for. If we get lucky, maybe we will see something we can use from the air. It never hurts to see the big picture."

The car wound along a two lane road through occasional little towns. McCabe eventually stopped at a diner in a small town for lunch. "This place has great cheeseburgers," he said.

"Now you're my dietician I guess too" said Montgomery, getting out of the truck. Her nice figure and new fashion drew looks from a couple of guys walking by on the sidewalk.

The small diner was a quaint change from what she was used to in San Antonio. A pleasant waitress promptly asked them what they would like.

She took their order. "Two cheese burger baskets and a side of rings. Would you like anything to drink?"

"Just water for me, thanks," responded McCabe.

"I'll have coffee, please."

She brought the coffee pot and a cup over and poured Shelly a cup.

"Thank you."

McCabe thought about the investigation for a moment.

"Tomorrow we should check in with the Jackson police and setup a plane ride over the lake. You can meet the local cops. Maybe they have heard something since I last talked to them."

The waitress brought them their burgers. "Anything else I can get you?" she asked politely.

They both shook their heads no and started in on the burgers.

"These are good," responded Shelly. "Nice waitress and good service too. So this is the Minnesota nice I have heard about?"

"This is it," said McCabe taking a bite of the juicy burger. "I told you it was a good place."

"Once again you are right on Jack."

After finishing lunch they were back on the road again. The car passed Superior national forest.

"We are in big woods country now. It is easy to get turned around and lost in this stuff. It happens to people all the time. One of the things I should have gotten you at that store was a hand held GPS unit. I have one but if we got split up in the woods you might need it. We can pick you up a compass in Jackson. They can really help get you out too. At least you don't walk in circles. Just stay with me and it won't be a problem. If you get lost with nothing, you could walk fifty miles or more through the woods before hitting a road sometimes."

She thought about that for a moment. "I did have survival training in the military before becoming an FBI special agent. I was in the Army."

"Really, I am learning more about you every day. Well I have been a hunter in these woods since I was a kid, and I still get lost in them sometimes. It is very easy to do, so it is good you have had some official training." He smiled at her.

"Did you have to eat worms and plants to prove you could survive off the land?"

Shelly laughed out loud remembering.

"Actually, I had to taste one worm at base camp and spend a night on the ground with a couple of other girls in the hills of Tennessee. It was a hoot. One of them smuggled in a pint of bourbon and we split it. We made a camp fire and told girl stories. It was pretty easy."

"Well if you have to spend a night up here alone, you might not find it as pleasant. There are things in these woods that can kill you. Not to mention our suspect roaming around," replied McCabe.

"Yeah, it was pretty light training for sure. I think they were harder on the guys. That was before women were going into combat situations. I bet that has all changed."

"I suppose so. Anyhow, up here the number one rule is to not wander around the woods in the dark. It is warm enough by day in late May, but you will still get cold at night. It can be thirty two degrees or less at night. You can get hypothermic without protection if it's a cold night. They say to gather firewood and make your camp a couple hours before it starts getting dark."

McCabe continued to instruct her in a very serious manner.

"Just make a fire and hunker down next to a tree until daybreak. If you can't make a fire, just sit under a big pine tree for rain protection. If you move in the black of night you could fall off a cliff. Then you have big problems if you break a leg or worse."

"Thanks for the information, Jack. Should I start calling you Mad Jack, the north woodsman? You really seem to know the ways of the forest," she responded sarcastically.

"I would hate to fall down in the woods and not be able to get up. Just like those poor elderly people in TV commercials. Maybe I should have woods alert while I am up here. Do they make that for people who fall down in the woods and can't get up? It would be like living in the woods alone but never being alone. How nice. I appreciate your concern, but I don't plan on getting lost anyway."

"Very funny, but if you do get lost, just remember what I said."

The car rolled down a hill past a sign saying Jackson, eight miles.

"We are going down into the lake basin now. You will see some views of the lake pretty soon. You can't see across it in some areas."

Soon the small resort town of Jackson appeared nestled at the edge of the big lake. Resort signs and marina activity marked the entrance into town. McCabe drove through the little town and headed north along the west side of the lake toward Flanagan's Resort.

As he passed the beach in town he pointed. "They found quite a few of the bodies near this beach."

"How come you think he is on the north end then?" she asked.

"Every time I have ever visited this lake over the years, the wind is always coming from the north. I am sure sometimes it is not, but I think the bodies washed up here from the waves."

"Good theory, I guess. I hope we're not on the wrong end of this lake. You were not kidding when you said it was huge."

"There is a river coming in from the north which also makes some current. I hope I am not wrong either, but I have no clues from anybody I talked to around here," said McCabe.

The car curved along the shoreline past some of the resorts McCabe had asked questions at.

"This is near where the guy told me about the big dude on the ice. He said it was on the other side by the state forest public landing."

"How far across is it to the other side?" asked Montgomery.

"I would say about ten miles across and about forty miles long. I want to fly over that public landing. This time I'm going to rent a bigger faster boat. I had a small fishing boat last time. I never got over to the landing as it was too far away."

"Then those two guys showed up dead in their boat and that took the rest of my time before I came down to meet you."

Soon they were on the northwest corner of the lake approaching Flanagan's Resort. As they bounced down the rough road into the resort McCabe looked at her.

"Let's just say you're my significant other if they say anything at the check in desk."

She laughed out loud. "Gee, will they let us in? This makes me feel like I am eighteen years old or something. Maybe we should find a justice of the peace and get married."

McCabe looked at her and smiled.

"Don't scare me away now girl. We are on a case working undercover. Don't forget about our mission."

"Yeah, we are under the covers alright," she replied.

The cool lake air made her put on a sweatshirt as she got out of the car. "Brrr.. It is cold."

McCabe rang the bell at the check in desk and Mrs. Flannigan appeared. "Welcome back Mr. Jack McCabe. I see you have a guest this time too."

"Hello Mrs. Flanagan. I will take the same cabin again if it is open. This is Shelly Montgomery."

She nodded to her and got the key for McCabe. Don't forget to sign our guestbook now."

"Oh, and you can put me down for a bundle of wood. We are going to try the fireplace," said McCabe with a smile.

"No problem. The firewood is right outside the cabin. Free of charge. Wood is the one thing we have a lot of up here. Too much woods, if you ask me," she said shaking her head.

They checked into the cozy cabin and McCabe got a fire started in the fireplace. Before long it was cozy warm and Shelly was sipping a glass of wine. Dusk was falling across the lake now and the wind calmed down.

"This is really incredible. I have never done anything like this before. It is very nice and peaceful."

The loons began to sing across the water.

"What is that noise?" she asked.

"That is our state bird the loon, and quite a singer I might add."

"It sounds so lonely and wild."

Another loon made a haunting call from the nearby shore.

"That is the wild call of the loon. They do that when they are looking for their mates."

Shelly looked at him and took a sip of wine. "I wonder if that is the male or female calling out."

"It's hard to say. I think the males do it more though."

"Why doesn't that surprise me Jack? Maybe that is the way things are supposed to be."

The firelight flickered in the now semi-dark room. McCabe added another log and sat down next to her.

"You are absolutely right on that." He put his arm around her.

As the night fell on the cabin, a lonely howl from a pack of timber wolves echoed across the lake. The wild country was a romantic setting indeed.

11

Montgomery awoke to the sun filtering through the window of the cabin. Jack was nowhere to be found. She saw a pot of fresh brewed coffee in the kitchen and poured herself a cup.

He must have gone up to the restaurant for breakfast, she thought. She showered and dressed quickly to look for McCabe.

As she left the cabin, she saw him fishing from the dock. She walked down the path to a beautiful sunrise on the lake. McCabe threw a long cast with an artificial lure as she approached.

"Good morning Jack. Do you always run out on your dates before the sun rises?"

"Only when I am on a fantastic lake like this one," he responded.

He opened the live well door to show her a nice seven pound northern pike swimming in the tank.

"Would you like fresh fish for supper tonight?"

"Wow, nice catch. Do you know how to make it?

"Don't need to. Just give it to the cook and they will clean it and prepare it for us tonight. Of course there is a slight fee but that is what vacations are all about."

"So now we are on vacation?" she laughed. "I thought we were here to catch a killer."

"We are and that's why I don't have time to do this myself. After breakfast we need to talk to Sheriff Campbell." After a quick meal they were back on the road to the town of Jackson. McCabe phoned Sheriff Campbell on the way.

"This is Sheriff Campbell speaking."

"Hello Sheriff, Jack McCabe, FBI."

"Hey Jack, how is it going? Captain Becker phoned me and told me you figured out who we are looking for. Nice work."

"Thanks, we believe we have identified him and he is linked to about a dozen murders in Texas as well."

"So, what do you need from us to help assist in finding him?" Campbell's attitude toward McCabe seemed to be much more accommodating, in light of the progress made on the case the last few days.

"For starters, we want to take a surveillance flight over the lake. You can come with us if you want and I can brief you on what we have."

"I am one of the local search and rescue pilots, so I will take you up personally. We have a float plane harbored in the marina. Looks like a good day for a plane ride."

"Okay, I can trust you not to do any military trick flying or anything, right?" McCabe responded joking.

"I also have a partner along who was working on the case in San Antonio. We can both go up, right?"

"Not a problem. We can seat four passengers plus gear. No worry on the flight either, these big float planes can't do barrel rolls so you are safe with me," he responded.

"We will meet you at the marina in about thirty minutes then?"

"Okay, I will see you down there."

As McCabe's truck wound through the outskirts of Jackson, he looked at Shelly.

"He appears to be in a good mood today. Please don't start showing him your switchblade and other toys."

"It is a stiletto Jack. The blade comes straight out and don't worry. I will keep it completely professional."

"Good, he was a little cranky and stressed from all this murder activity last time I talked to him."

As they walked out on the marina dock the Sheriff was removing tie down anchors from the plane.

"Thanks for helping with this Sheriff. This is my partner, special agent Shelly Montgomery. She is the chief investigator on our suspect who appears to be also involved in the San Antonio River Walk murders."

She held out her handshake to the Sheriff.

"I'm pleased to meet you Sheriff. It sounds like you have had your hands full with this guy too."

Campbell shook her hand. "Yes, we certainly have."

As they climbed into the plane and taxied out on to the big lake for takeoff, McCabe started to brief him on the case.

"The guy's name is Tom Jepson, an ex-con and ruthless cannibal. We believe he is probably living off the land somewhere around here."

"Your boss told me he was in military prison for trying to secede from the union with a survivalist group," responded Campbell.

"I saw a few of those types when I was in the military police."

McCabe looked at him as the plane moved along slowly.

"Well he has taken it a step further than just being a rebel. He is now a confirmed crazy cannibal feeding off people when he has to get food. We have reason to believe he was eating some of those people who washed up last winter to survive."

"Jesus, that's new ground for me chasing after someone like that," said a slightly astonished Sheriff.

Campbell pushed down the throttle and the plane accelerated loudly as the engine reached takeoff speed. Once airborne the plane rose over the large expanse of water and surrounding woods.

"So where do you want to go first?"

McCabe pointed up to the north east corner of the lake.

"Can you fly up the east shoreline? I have already seen the west side of the lake pretty good from my car and boat."

As the plane gained altitude you could see the lakes and rivers surrounded by trees. Shelly looked out the window in awe.

"You were not kidding about the Land of 10,000 Lakes, were you?

"I told you it would be a cool view." responded her partner. McCabe looked at the Sheriff. "How low can we fly?"

Campbell smiled, "All depends on how safe you want to be if we have mechanical problems. Usually we go about a couple thousand feet over the woods. I can go lower though if we stay close to the water. These planes don't glide the greatest with floats on them. When you start losing power you come down pretty fast."

He brought the plane down to about five hundred feet flying along the east shoreline. "That is Superior National forest to the far north. It is a huge chunk of woods. It's about four million acres of land and water. About a quarter of that is Boundary Waters Canoe Wilderness, where people travel across interconnected lakes and rivers and over land portages once used by the early fur traders. No motorized vehicles are allowed including restricted fly zones for airplanes. Much of it's very remote. The rest of the forest is pretty much used for recreational lakes, camping, fishing, boating and some logging operations. The northeast corner of the lake is the Indian reservation which we will be flying over soon.

As the plane skimmed the tree tops it allowed a good view of the shoreline below. The plane crossed over an open area and a road to the lake's edge.

"That is the public landing down there. It's not used a whole lot. It is a long way in from the highway on a washboard gravel road. Once in a while someone pulls their boat in and tries fishing the north side. Usually just fishermen with smaller boats use it."

"If you have a big boat that can handle the waves, it is easier to put in at the Jackson landing. Then drive up to the north side by boat if you want to fish up here."

McCabe and Montgomery scanned the area for anything they might be able to work with. All they could see were the tree tops. McCabe continued to brief the Sheriff.

"This guy is also a hawker, a guy who hunts with birds. He is into birds of prey and trains them."

He did not mention what had happened to him. The reservation town on Rice Bay appeared over the tree tops.

"My personal belief is that he is in this area somewhere."

"Why is that?" Campbell looked at him inquisitively.

"Because I have interviewed some of the local Indians and I just have a hunch somebody might have hired him to scare people away from the north end of the lake."

"Well if that is the case, he is sure doing a good job of it."

Shelly Montgomery continued to stare out the window as they were talking. Suddenly she interjected into the conversation.

"What is that? I just saw something on the shoreline," she said.

McCabe turned to look down but it was too late.

"It was something shining. Like a hidden boat or something. Circle around for another look. It was in that little bay by the beaver pond."

Campbell circled the plane back for another look. As the aircraft approached the bay, a glint of aluminum flashed from behind the beaver pond.

"That looks like a stashed canoe," said McCabe.

"It could be an Indian setting up for the rice gathering season or maybe setting up a trap line," said Campbell.

"Or maybe it could be how Jepson is moving around the shoreline," said McCabe. "Fly over it again. I want to see what that is for sure."

Campbell revved the engine and dove in a swoop on the object taking the plane right over it at about two hundred feet up. You could see the outline of a canoe covered with bulrushes.

"Somebody is hiding that thing," said Montgomery.

McCabe looked up and saw a hawk circling to his right. "Maybe nothing, maybe something, we will check it out later."

The plane continued over the reservation and some high cliffs on the north side of the lake. There were very few breaks in the trees as the plane zoomed over the reservation land.

An occasional cabin or small house would appear with a cleared yard. By and large the land was not cleared of woods and the view was limited. When you looked at the horizon all you could see were tree tops and blue water to the north.

"Can you take us way up high once over this area for a big view? Shelly has never seen the lake country."

"No problem," Campbell circled the plane around the reservation to three thousand feet.

"This is an awesome view," responded Shelly.

"I just want you to get a perspective on how big these woods really are. Like I was telling you in the car, you can get turned around and lose your sense of direction," said McCabe.

"That is for sure," said Campbell.

"We pull quite a few out of these woods every year. Most are hopelessly lost and usually close to being hypothermic and half starved by the time we find them. It still gets cold at night in the summer. This time of year in the spring, it is still in the high thirties at night. Even in mid summer the lows are in the forties and fifties. Sometimes even lower."

The airplane's high altitude showed how far one could have to walk if lost.

"See that road way over on the right?" said Campbell.

"That is seven miles from the lake. If you had to walk from the lake to the road through the bush, it would be more like twenty miles. That is, following a compass and going around obstacles like flooded beaver ponds in a zigzag path."

He went on explaining.

"If you go in circles, a five mile woods can hold you for days. A ten mile stretch you might never get out on your own if you can't stay on a semi straight line."

The plane flew west over Flanagan's tavern. "We are staying at Flanagan's Resort if you are looking for us," said McCabe.

"So what is your next move?" asked Campbell.

"I thought we would do some light investigating around Rice Bay. Check out that canoe and walk some trails. Take a look at the public landing and see if we think this guy is still around," said McCabe.

Campbell looked at them both. "We have two bloodhound dogs and I can put together a search team if you want."

McCabe responded. "I appreciate the offer Sheriff. I think if we find something we will take you up on it. If he is here we don't want him to flee the area. I don't want to scare him off."

"I can understand that," said Campbell.

"Just be careful. Tracking an armed man in the woods is big time dangerous. I had to do it in Vietnam and once up here. The guy shot one of our German shepherds and wounded a deputy. A guy with a gun in the woods who knows what he is doing is not any easy capture. In fact, the guys tracking him are an easy mark if he sets up like a sniper. Be careful."

McCabe acknowledged his warning.

"Thanks Sheriff, I appreciate the advice and if we get something going with this guy, I will bring you in. I could use your expertise. We want this guy bad but we don't have to get killed over it either. He's going to make a mistake on the lake if we wait long enough."

Campbell nodded his head. "If you find evidence your man is out there we will get a pack of hounds on him. Just be careful, and don't get lost. We really don't want to have to do a search and rescue on you two. Especially with that nut potentially in the woods while we are looking for you."

McCabe nodded in agreement.

"Much appreciated Sheriff. We will be careful and we might need those dogs. If we do, we will setup a police net of the surrounding area first. Then bring in dogs and man power to flush him out. If he runs to the surrounding roads, we should be able to still get him with police road blocks."

"Sounds kind of like a text book military plan. I just hope this guy behaves like a text book psychopath for your sake," said Campbell.

The Sheriff landed the plane on the smooth lake surface and taxied up to the dock in Jackson. As they climbed out, Sheriff Campbell shook their hands, wishing them good luck.

Thanking him for the ride, they started walking up the dock to the parking lot.

"Call me now if you need reinforcements. Don't forget we are right here for you on this one. We want to catch this guy as bad as anyone," shouted Campbell.

McCabe waved and climbed into his truck. "I really think he wants to come along," he said kind of laughing. We very well might need a guy just like him before this is over. I hope he stays enthusiastic about it."

12

While driving back to the resort, they discussed their next move. McCabe pulled into a scenic overlook on the lake and took in the view across the lake. "Tomorrow morning I would like to drive over and look around the landing," he said.

"Maybe check out that hidden canoe, too."

Shelly nodded in agreement. "Yeah, that seems kind of odd that someone would hide a boat like that in the weeds."

"Actually, people who portage from lake to lake do that sometimes, so it is not really all that uncommon. But you never know. I just have a feeling about that part of the lake. Maybe it is the old Indian legend getting to me or something. I'm not sure."

McCabe put his arm around Shelly and gave her a kiss. "It is going to be a beautiful day. Let's have a little fun on the lake and barbecue this afternoon."

"That sounds like a great idea. If the Griffin has been hiding in the woods since winter, he will more than likely be hiding out all summer. He must have a good hideout. As I said before, all work and no play makes Jack a dull boy."

McCabe pulled out of the scenic overlook as a speed boat clipped along the water below. Heading toward Flanagan's road the temperature continued to rise as the noon hour approached. By the time they reached the resort the car thermometer had reached eighty degrees.

A warm front from the south pushed in beautiful late spring weather. The lake had already come alive with boaters taking advantage of the warm temperatures.

"You were right Jack. Last night was freezing and this afternoon it is super nice out. This weather is weird."

"It can change like the wind for sure. When you live in the north, the first warm day is so fun. Everybody is in a fantastic mood when this kind of weather hits."

McCabe poured charcoal into the grill near the dock.

"This is what the people up here live for. That first hot day on the lake is awesome. It's like you have waited so long for summer it just does something to your spirit. You can even get in the water if you are tough enough. Look at that guy water skiing."

A boat raced by off shore pulling a slalom skier who was carving big spray to the sides of the boat. McCabe smiled at the sight. "That guy probably took off right from the dock. If you are good enough you don't have to be in the water very long."

Shelly opened a beer and looked at all the activity. A big pontoon boat pulled up to Flanagan's dock. A boisterous crowd of young people obviously having a good time unloaded and went inside.

"This is incredible. The place seemed deserted last night and this morning. It is boating central now. Plus it is such a big lake there is still plenty of room to get away from other boats if you want. When the first warm day hits on a Texas lake, you can almost walk across it on boats. It is almost scary when people start zooming around like that guy. Collisions can and do happen sometimes."

McCabe lit the coals and pulled a beer out of the cooler. "Collisions and accidents can happen here as well, but they hardly ever do. You are more apt to hit a rock in low water conditions than another boat. Especially on lakes like this one which has lots of islands and boulders. When the water level goes down a few feet, rocks start popping up on the surface. It's the boulders right below the surface you need to worry about. Most are marked but it can be risky outside the main channels in late summer.

The sun was beginning to set as they sat on lawn chairs near the dock overlooking the beautiful lake. The first loon made an evening cry and the chorus began.

"Now, this is the life Shelly. Here we are on a beautiful pristine lake with the sun setting on a warm evening. We've got steaks ready to sizzle on the grill, a beer in hand and the loons are starting to sing. I hate to sound corny with the old cliché, but it really doesn't get any better than this."

Shelly sat on his lap. "It is really beautiful. I am so glad you brought me up here."

McCabe smiled at her. "When I add your gorgeous presence into this picture it makes my last statement especially true."

"And aren't you the smooth talking ladies man."

"Not at all sweetheart, it just comes natural to me when I am with you."

"Mr. Jack McCabe. Hot shot northern based FBI agent falling in love with a south Texas girl. Isn't that a sweet and romantic love story? And after we catch this guy, it will probably be back to work as usual for old Jack. I suppose I won't hear from you for quite awhile."

McCabe hugged her. “Don’t be so glum Shelly. I just might surprise you. You know, I want kids and all that stuff just like everyone else someday.”

She chuckled. “I am not so sure a McCabe can reproduce in captivity though. You don’t seem like the marrying type.”

“Once again, I might just surprise you, beautiful.”

“Okay Jack, I won’t hold my breath practicing the name Shelly McCabe though. I think I know you better than yourself sometimes.”

McCabe kissed her again and picked her up in his arms. “I am not going to carry you across a threshold, so relax. I just want to go get some potatoes and carrots going.”

Shelly shook her head laughing as he put her down and walked up to the cabin. Now that is a romantic guy she thought. And he likes to cook too.

McCabe appeared from the cabin door shortly with a tinfoil concoction of chopped potatoes, carrots, onions, and peppers.

“This is how we barbecue northern style. Or, maybe I should say McCabe style. Just throw these on the grill with a little water and butter in the tin foil and let them simmer on the coals.”

“How long do you cook them for?”

McCabe grinned at her. “About three beers and they should be perfect.”

Once again she smiled and shook her head at her man’s cooking methods. A typical male mentality, she thought. She envied the fact that they could be so relaxed and unstructured. Almost as if they had a built in blind stupidity to the possibility of ruining the meal from over cooking. An incredible species, she thought as she watched him work the tin foil.

“On my third beer I usually start the steaks. Cooking is all about timing.”

She laughed at him. “Is that why you never use a watch? I suppose that would not be accurate enough.”

“That would seem like way too much work keeping track of the time. It is more challenging going by your instincts. That’s the sign of a true master barbecue man.”

As they enjoyed the sunshine, Jack cooked the steaks to perfection with his unusual methods. After a nice steak dinner on the lake they proceeded to Flanagan's bar at dusk.

The idea was to gather possible information from the locals and have a good time. Not necessarily in that order. As they entered the bar there were a number of people on stage enjoying karaoke night.

Jack and Shelly eased up to the bar and ordered a couple of beers. Around the bar Jack saw one familiar face in George White Owl. He walked over and said hello to Jack with an added interest in his attractive female friend.

"Hello, Jack McCabe. Have you been staying clear of the eagles in Rice Bay?"

Jack held out his hand. "Hi George, this is my friend Shelly Montgomery. Shelly, this is George White Owl. He lives on the reservation across the lake."

White Owl shook her extended hand and smiled.

"Are you from around this area?" he asked. I have never seen you here before."

"This is the first time here, Mr. White Owl. I am actually on vacation from San Antonio, Texas."

White Owl smiled at her and responded. "I love Texas. I make runs with my semi truck down to the Brownsville area several times a year. I have always thought the Mexican women were very pretty."

Jack looked at her and kind of shook his head. Shelly responded, "So what kind of cargo do you transport, Mr. White Owl?"

"I pretty much transport anything that is profitable to haul. That usually means light cargo is best. But mostly I haul freight for any company that wants my services, provided I do not need to load or unload it on the pickup or delivery side."

"I guess that's the life of an independent trucker. I suppose it gets lonely on the road," said Shelly.

White Owl smiled and moved closer to her. "As long as I have Mexican beauties like you around me, I do just fine passing the time."

At that point Jack interceded and asked Shelly to dance. The beers were flowing and several couples danced to the slow karaoke song. Fortunately, it was being sung by a talented female vocalist.

"That guy kind of gives me the creeps," said Shelly.

Jack agreed that he seemed maybe a little out of line.

"I think he is pretty harmless but I wouldn't recommend getting too friendly. He couldn't take his eyes off you. I can hardly blame him though as I seem to have the same problem."

As the night carried on they discussed last winter's murders briefly but mostly kept the conversation light. One of the guys at the bar had mentioned a big dude in a canoe at the public landing a few days ago.

His description was basically a very large man in primitive clothing. Like something right out of the 1800s wearing buckskin clothing. He thought maybe he was from a local renaissance festival or something.

Jack did not acknowledge that the description pretty much matched the profile of the Griffin. He did not want to alarm people to the possibility of a mad man stalking the lake. Plus nobody in the bar knew they were Federal agents.

Before long, the people around the bar began taking turns singing karaoke songs. It was pretty entertaining as the crowd was getting less inhibited with the alcohol intake.

Apparently, Flanagan's karaoke machine was the Friday night entertainment. He rarely hired bands as the customers could provide decent singing and plenty of laughter for free.

The more they drank, the better the effort to become a temporary rock star. The bad performances were the best ones to laugh at. All participants were on their honor to give it their best shot even if they couldn't sing a simple tune. Some with the worst voices made up for it with dance moves and acting. Good humor to say the least.

Eventually it was Jack and Shelly's turn and the bar crowd urged them onto the stage with vocal persuasion. Finally they agreed and they chose a duet of the song "Fever" originally sung by Johnny and June Cash.

They had fun with the song. They were obviously not masters of the tune like Johnny and June, but had a good time belting out the song. Shelly wondered if they ever would get married in a "Fever" like the song stated. The crowd roared approval as they sang the song in perfect unison, gaining confidence as it went on.

They had so much fun they even did an encore performance and sang it even better the second time around. They were both Johnny Cash fans so they knew the words well.

Eventually, they closed the place down. At one point Jack had to sit George White Owl down as he kept making passes at his girl. George divulged to Shelly that he always tries to pick up Mexican senoritas as he absolutely loves Mexican women.

Shelly laughed as Jack put his arm around a drunken George White Owl and had a man to man talk with him. A real counselor, she mused as they both appeared pretty intoxicated.

She was glad he did intervene, as White Owl was starting to annoy her with his stupid banter about Mexican girls. Sometimes he said he gave poor girls rides in his truck. She could imagine this creep driving around down by the border cruising for young Mexican girls needing a place to stay.

White Owl seemed odd to her. Something was strange about him. Something more than just being a drunken aging man who seemed to liked Mexican girls a little too much.

His occasional comments made her think he was a bit of a pervert. He had a cold degrading demeanor when he spoke of women in his life, especially when he spoke of the females he would meet around the Mexican border.

He was probably just a big liar and wishing the ladies liked him. In reality, she found him quite unattractive and doubted his proclaimed exploits as a famed ladies' man. He seemed to think he was a real Don Juan in every Mexican border town between Brownsville and Laredo.

As the night drew to a close, they both said their good nights to new friends at the tavern and left the door arm in arm.

"Now that was a pretty good time," said Jack.

Shelly responded, "Except for that White Owl creep it was pretty fun." She pondered the evening encounter for a moment.

"There is something strange about that guy. I think we should investigate him further. He has some real fantasies and made a point of trying to impress me with his stories. Considering DNA tests show all but one of the bodies in this case was of Hispanic decent, something does not seem right with him."

Jack agreed, "I was thinking the same thing. He also is the one who told me about the Indian curse. It might be nothing but you never know in cases like this. Most of those girls are Mexican and they got up here somehow. We'll look into his activities further for sure. But tomorrow we are going over to the boat landing. I like that tip about the guy in buckskin clothes."

Shelly nodded, "Yeah, he meets the description of our man. We might as well focus on him first."

As they stood on the cabin deck a loon sang from the nearby shoreline. Shelly put her arms around Jack and kissed him.

"I really love this life in the north woods Jack."

McCabe picked her up while still kissing her and carried her into the cabin across the threshold. "You are quite a woman. A lot of women would have been offended by some of the jokes getting thrown around in the place."

"I was offended a few times. They have just never seen me really pissed off or they would watch their mouths a little better. For that matter, you have never seen me really pissed off either."

"I will always avoid that situation Shelly. I don't want you doing your karate shit on me."

As he lit the fire and poured her a glass of wine he turned to her. "I suppose I still have a lot to learn about you."

"Well Jack, I hope I am not so simple you have me all figured out in a couple of weeks."

She walked over to him and put her arms around him.

"I think we are making a good start though. Maybe we shouldn't think about it so much and just let it happen."

Jack looked into her eyes and smiled. Reaching over he shut off the light. "You are an awesome woman and smarter than you look too."

They toppled over to the bed in each other's arms laughing. Jack could always make her laugh with his idiotic phrases. She whacked him one for the last crack.

The full moonlight coursed through the window as the loons sang their romantic songs. Tomorrow would be another beautiful day in the northland. Another day to savor the bliss of their blossoming relationship and work as partners tracking a killer in the north woods.

13

The Griffin awoke from his drunken slumber as dusk was settling on the bay. He peered out on the water and saw a boat drifting with its navigational lights on. He picked up a pair of binoculars and zoomed in on the boat license.

He was doing as the Indian man had instructed. The reservation boats had a special identification sticker. This drifting boat did not have the sticker. He spoke to his wolf dog.

"He is not Indian and floats on their water. We must carry out the curse and please the gods."

He watched the man drift across the bay. The wind pushed him close to the shoreline near the Griffin's canoe. "This intruder floats close to our shores. It is time. We shall show him our hospitality."

From the floor of the cave he picked up his rifle and headed down to the lake. Crossing the marsh he uncovered his canoe and watched the man from behind the beaver hut. He softly spoke to his dog.

"How should we take this one Lobo? Maybe you would like to kill him this time. Or, I could just paddle up and shoot him dead. That would be too easy though. We should keep him alive and play with him as long as we can, like a game of cat and mouse. He can entertain us and eventually feed us. Let's see how stupid and meek these unsuspecting humans really are."

He pushed the canoe though the reeds and began paddling towards the man's drifting boat. Lobo sat in the front intently eyeing the drifting watercraft. They are very gullible he thought. He would paddle close to him. He would paddle right up and talk to him. He would paddle up and attack him with his bare hands.

The Griffin pondered his method of attack as the boat came closer. Even with all the recent lake killings, the fisherman in Rice Bay could only focus on fishing. He will believe in the Indian curse when I have finished with him.

He wanted this one alive. He had enjoyed his live encounter with the two fishermen he had killed earlier in the season. He brought those two men to his cave at gun point. This time he would not use his gun.

The canoe made a line toward the drifting boat and closed to within three hundred feet. The fisherman was drifting right at the Griffin's canoe. The man was totally unaware of the Griffin's canoe and continued concentrating on his fishing.

Casting crank baits and retrieving them rapidly, his focus was on not getting his lure snagged in the heavy weed beds three feet below the water's surface. The fisherman was glad the approaching boat was a canoe so it would not spook the fish. Canoes were a common site on Tanner's Lake. The lake was an official entry point into the Boundary Waters Canoe Area (BWCA) by portage. A portage trail from the northeast shore of Tanner's Lake connected to the Kawishiwi river system. From there you could travel anywhere in the BWCA. Lakes dotted the area and portage trails connected them all the way to Canada.

Canoe travel was not much different than the French Fur traders of the early 1800s. All motorized power was restricted after Tanner's Lake, so it was the only method of travel in the wilderness. Canoes in the summer and dog sleds in the winter were the best methods of travel. State hiking trails were also used frequently by those who preferred foot travel.

As the canoe approached, the fisherman got a better look at the Griffin. This guy looked like he had been in the wilderness for quite some time. Probably paddling back to Flanagan's resort, he thought.

He had done trips of two weeks in the Boundary Waters Wilderness and remembered how good it felt to get back to his car and civilization. It was great to get away from it all, but sleeping on the ground got old after awhile. It could be a tough but also rewarding trip spending time in the wilderness.

The large man was dressed in animal skins and appeared like an animal himself. As he drifted closer, the fisherman finally took notice and spoke. "Howdy, I bet you're coming out of the Boundary Waters Canoe Area."

The Griffin just stared at him as the fishing boat continued drifting now within twenty feet and closing. It looked as if a collision was about to happen. The man in the boat stood up and moved toward his boat controls.

The close up sight of the Griffin was somewhat disturbing and the tone of the fisherman's voice changed. The boats moved together in seconds. There was a slightly nervous inflection as the fisherman spoke.

"Nice dog, what kind of dog is that?"

The Griffin remained silent. He swung the canoe within two feet of the side of the fishing boat, just missing the transom.

The fisherman saw the rifle propped next to the Griffin in the canoe. He knew there were no open hunting seasons in the spring in northern Minnesota. He also noticed the man had no packs or gear in the canoe.

The fisherman spoke as the canoe positioned itself next to his boat.

"Sorry, I didn't mean to throw your canoe off course. I know it is not easy paddling against the waves. I bet you're heading back to Flanagan's resort."

The Griffin said nothing and lunged at the man grabbing the side of his boat. His dog jumped across into the boat attacking the fisherman as the Griffin climbed aboard.

Obviously shocked, the man jumped back as the dog snarled and lunged at him. The man threw the biting dog overboard into the lake. The animal lost his grip on his forearm as it was flung overboard into the water. The dog hit the water with a splash. Blood ran down the fisherman's forearm from the vicious bite he had just received.

When he looked up he saw the dog's master.

The Griffin was now aboard and spoke.

"He is a killer dog. That's what kind of dog he is. The dog is half Wolf and half Great Dane. I will feed your heart to him for supper tonight. He has a big appetite and I must feed him well."

Shocked at the sight of him, the man was terrified. The Griffin's six foot six frame moved toward him. The fisherman stood at the bow of the boat holding his torn and bleeding arm.

The dog was swimming in the water next to the boat. He thought of jumping, but feared the animal in the water. He decided to stand his ground. He grabbed the boat anchor at his feet in the bow.

"What do you want? Get off of my boat!"

The Griffin just smiled and slowly walked toward the man.

Throwing the fifteen pound boat anchor at the approaching monster, he landed a glancing blow off his shoulder. The Griffin winced in pain for a moment but continued moving forward. In a matter of seconds, he had the fisherman by the throat.

His strong right arm and large muscular hand squeezed the smaller man, dropping him to his knees. He flailed his arms at the Griffin but his blows seemed to just bounce off the deer skin poncho. He was physically no match for the Griffin, who towered over him.

The Griffin laughed at the fisherman's feeble fight. His crazed eyes pierced the choking man, looking directly into his eyes.

"You should not fish on the Indian land my friend. You must not be able to read your fishing regulations. I am the enforcer of the bay. I am enforcer of the legend. I am Prometheus the Griffin. I am a Titan."

The Griffin lifted his victim off the floor of the boat with his choking hand. He continued to choke the life from the man as he stared into his eyes until he blacked out. The fisherman struggled violently for a moment before losing consciousness.

The Griffin released his grip and the man fell to the floor. Alive but unconscious, the Griffin would keep him that way until he was ready to use him. The hulking man reached over the bow and hoisted in the swimming dog. Once in the boat, the dog instantly tore into the unconscious man's leg.

The Griffin swatted the dog off with a canoe paddle. The dog snarled at him and the Griffin stared him down in dominance. The dog backed off and sat in the end of the boat.

"Don't worry my four footed friend, you will get your share. We must feed everyone off this carcass."

He tied the canoe to the fishing boat and drove it back to the bay. He maneuvered the boat deep into the reeds of Rice Bay and beached it in about three feet of water. We will camouflage this later, he thought.

The hulking man picked up his prisoner who was slowly regaining consciousness. He threw him over his shoulder like a sack of potatoes and started up the trail to the cave.

"We will keep you fresh and eat you as slow as possible my friend. Keeping you alive is just like having a refrigerator in the woods."

He chuckled as his prize groaned and struggled momentarily. He pulled the man down and struck him hard in the face. Tossing him back over his shoulder, he thought how easy it was to catch men instead of animals. It was much easier and less dangerous than a struggling whitetail deer in one of his pits. When he reached the cave entrance he threw the dazed man to the ground.

"If you make noise I will cut your tongue out right now."

The terrified man was staked out with limbs extended on the ground. The Griffin gagged the man just to make sure he was quiet. He did not really want to cut his tongue, as it might kill him. If he bled to death the meat would spoil. It would be better to have some small meals and then a big feast at the end.

From the cave, the Griffin pulled out a camouflaged tarp and walked down to the fisherman's boat. First he pulled the plug on the boat and let it completely fill with water. Throwing large rocks in the bottom of the boat, he sunk it to the lake bottom in four feet of water.

He tied the camouflaged tarp to the submerged boat frame and strategically placed some reeds up and around it. This made it virtually invisible from the air. He knew the police would search for the boat by airplane when the fisherman was reported missing.

Satisfied with the boats concealment, he returned to the cave and his prisoner. He sawed off two small chunks of flesh from the calf of each leg. His prisoner twisted and tried to scream as the cut was made.

"This will make you not run quite so fast when I cut you loose. It will also give us a blood trail to follow. Lobo is very good at following human blood trails. I want you to be able to run and make good sport for the game. You must have a fair chance to escape from the Griffin."

Returning to an outcropping of rock on the cave ledge, he held up both pieces of flesh he had just cut from the man's leg. With his long out stretched arms he dangled the flesh from his fingertips. With a loud screaming shriek he mimicked the scream of a dying rabbit. It was his call for the trained raptors. Soon both birds swooped in for their pieces of meat.

He spoke to his birds as they landed on their wooden stumps eating the flesh. They had seen men staked to the ground before and knew it meant food.

"My fine feathered friends, once again you will eat the flesh of the human. This time it will be different though. You must help me catch him. You will be my spotters in the sky."

He walked around the staked out man and kicked him in the ribs. The man groaned and cursed the Griffin in anger. He threw his head back in laughter as his victim cursed him.

"We are going to play a game with the human this evening. We are going to let him loose and practice our hunting skills."

The Griffin kicked him again and the man struggled hard to get loose. The prisoner spit at him and cursed him even more. The Griffin glared at him with crazed piercing eyes and spoke.

"I am tempted to just kill you and devour you right now, but my animals need the hunting practice. You, my friend, are nothing more than a wounded animal to them. They will track you, cripple you, and hold you for the Griffin."

The terrified man continued to curse and pull against his bound arms and legs.

The Griffin smiled in approval.

"That is good that you are showing some feisty behavior my friend. You will need it when we start the hunt. You will make fine sport for us all."

14

A beautiful sunrise broke across the bay from the east. Shelly climbed from her bed and the smell of fresh brewed coffee drifted through the cabin. Pouring a cup, she walked onto the cabin deck. The cool morning dew made everything wet and a bit cool. Putting on her wind breaker, she sipped her coffee and took in the magical beauty of the morning lake. The cool air made her feel alive. It was so different from the blazing hot mornings she was used to.

Jack was already down on the dock casting for northern pike. As the sun poked over the eastern tree line, fog from the cool night air rose from the lake's surface. Thick wisps of the fog cloud rose up off the lake surface in irregular patterns and shapes.

Loons called from behind the fog and flew back and forth splashing their wings along the water. She walked down to the dock and spoke to Jack.

"This morning fog is kind of eerie. Any luck fishing this morning?"

"Let one go about twenty minutes ago. Nice fish but in the slot. What a beautiful morning."

"So what adventure are we off on today Mr. McCabe?"

Jack smiled at her and gave her a hug.

"Today we are going to try and get a look at our killer and see what we are up against. It will take a little luck though. I will explain over breakfast in the restaurant."

Shelly returned to the cabin and prepared herself for the day. Once she was ready, they wandered up to get some food. As they sat down they were greeted by one of Flanagan's daughters working as morning waitress. She was working the bar last night as well.

"Hello, can I get you coffee?"

They both answered yes in unison. "A pot of coffee coming up."

Shelly put her hand to her forehead. "Coffee is a good thing after a night like last night. We made quite a duet in the singing competition."

Jack chuckled over the Johnny Cash tune they sang. "They might want us on American Idol if we're not careful."

The waitress returned. "Are you ready to order?"

Jack smiled at her, "I'll have number three, The Lumberjack, with whole wheat toast and a short stack of cakes."

He paused as she wrote down his order and then blurted out, "I was going to wear all black clothes today. Do you think I should?"

The waitress looked up and laughed.

"Sure Johnny, you look good in black. Maybe you can sing My Name is Sue tonight. Just don't cause any trouble. We don't like fights in Flanagan's bar."

Shelly shook her head at their banter. She couldn't help but laugh thinking about the karaoke. Jack really got into it.

The waitress turned to her. "And what can I get you June?"

Shelly broke out laughing. They were open game for teasing at this point.

"You can give me a number two with basted eggs, sausage and whole wheat toast. And I will take a Bloody Mary as well."

Jack perked up. "Make that two please. Whatever is good for June is good for Johnny. I guess we are on vacation."

She took their orders and returned with two Bloody Mary drinks, both with hefty celery sticks pointing upward from a large black pepper rimmed mug. Each drink had a small shot of beer chaser on the side.

"Now this is a good Bloody Mary," mused Jack. "Usually I don't go for a breakfast drink in the morning. However, it's almost high noon on the east coast, so I guess we're okay. Too bad we're not there. If we were, then it would be okay for sure."

Shelly laughed at his stupid reckoning. "Thanks for looking out for me Jack. I didn't know we were on a clock. Was I supposed to punch in this morning too? Normally as a good Mexican girl on a vacation, I would order a Tequila Sunrise instead, but for some reason a Bloody Mary sounded good."

Their food arrived shortly and they watched the fog burn off the lake surface as they enjoyed their hearty breakfast. "That fog looks really cool the way it climbs up off the water like that." Shelly had not really seen anything quite like that in South Texas.

"That's because the water is warmer than the night air. It got pretty cold last night. The sun should burn it off in an hour or so. It looks like it will be a really nice day."

Jack went on, "Sometimes you see that kind of fog in the winter on open water and it's really awesome. Lake Superior gets like that once in awhile in the dead of winter. It's so big it hardly ever freezes completely over. It can be minus twenty below zero air temperature with the water temperature in the mid thirty degree range. Steam just shoots up in spiraling circles across the skyline when the water is a lot warmer than the air."

The conversation eventually turned to the task at hand, which was locating Tom Jepson, alias the Griffin.

Jack laid out his plan to Shelly.

"I have five cameras in my truck which are used for taking pictures of wild game. They are camouflaged and detect motion. I want to plant a few around the landing and around that canoe in Rice Bay."

Shelly nodded her head. "Maybe we can ID him with a picture."

"That would be great if he tripped one. I also want to get in there on foot and see what we come across. There is a chance we could run into him if he's still around."

When breakfast was finished they loaded their boat with the gear they needed for the day. Jack loaded his shotgun in the boat along with the game cameras.

Shelly packed a lunch and cooler along with a bag containing her weapons. She carried a digital camera for photographs. She wanted pictures to remember the lake. Also, it would come in handy if they came across anything pertaining to the case.

Jack fired up the boat and untied it. After easing away from the dock he hit the throttle and sped across the lake toward the boat landing. His new rental boat was bigger and faster than the prior trip. More expensive to rent but they needed it this time. The one hundred eighty horse outboard pushed the seventeen foot fishing boat across the lake plenty fast. The boat also had a walk through windshield for wind and splash protection.

After about a five minute boat ride the far shoreline came into better view. As they eased along the eastern shore they saw the public landing and dock. Jack eased the boat up to the dock and tied it up. After moving the shotgun and other gear into the locked boat storage compartments, they climbed onto the dock.

The landing was deserted for the moment, except for an old beat up pickup truck parked off to one side in knee high weeds. It looked like it had not been driven for awhile. It was pointed up an old logging road.

Shelly looked up the rough trail. Deep tire ruts and mud puddles lined the muddy road. Jack walked back in the trees about fifteen yards and set up one of his cameras pointing at the truck. Shelly wrote down the truck license plate.

"Let's take a walk up this old road and see if we see anything."

Jack agreed, "Good day for a walk too."

As they headed up the trail it was a typical rough logging road. It appeared four wheelers had been on the road before too.

After about twenty minutes of walking, the trail narrowed and just sort of came to an end. It looked like there were a couple of rarely used foot trails moving off to the south. They might have even been deer trails.

Jack looked closely at the trail for prints in the ground. Deer were definitely using the trail for sure. He knew that they often used man made trails created through the thick underbrush as it was easier.

Jack stepped into the woods. "Let's follow this trail a little ways and see where it goes." Another step and a ruffed grouse exploded from the forest floor darting through the trees. Shelly jumped back about a foot as the bird's flush startled her.

Jack laughed as she regained her breath. "Don't feel bad. They still scare the crap out of me and I have been hunting them for twenty years."

Shelly followed behind him through the dense forest. "You were not kidding when you told me the woods got thick in the summertime. You never told me there were thunder birds in the forest."

Jack responded. "Actually you can see pretty good right now as the leaves are still small. Try this in July and you probably would not even see this trail. Or that grouse that just flushed."

Green ferns were sprouting everywhere along the trail. "These ferns will grow waist high by mid summer and be three feet across."

Jack got down on one knee and examined a muddy spot on the trail. He saw deer and what looked to be dog or wolf prints. They continued following the trail as the woods seemed to enclose around them. The trail seemed to get fainter and less traveled the further they went.

Finally, Jack spotted a boot print. Maybe a hunter, he thought. As they continued deeper into the woods they passed a deer stand and eventually the trail appeared to just end. Looking high in the sky he noticed what appeared to be an eagle circling overhead.

He pointed it out to Shelly. "There is an eagle circling above us."

"Maybe it is your buddy the attack bird."

Jack looked around and noticed something off to his right. He walked off the trail about ten yards. Peering through the trees, he was able to faintly make out the shape of a building structure.

"Shelly, check this out."

Shelly walked in where Jack was standing. "Do you see that?" Shelly gazed into the brown and green forest. "Do I see what?"

"Follow me."

As he went another twenty yards deeper into the woods, the outline of an old grey shack was now becoming apparent. "It looks like an old abandoned hunting shack."

Jack put his finger to his lips motioning Shelly to be silent. They both drew their revolvers. Jack motioned Shelly to flank him on the left and stay back while he took a look.

McCabe approached cautiously just in case it was the Griffin's hideout. Peering through a broken window he could see no one was there. He circled the small shack and motioned Shelly to come in.

They opened the door and went inside. This was not a typical deer shack. This was something else. You could tell somebody had been there not long ago. Hunting traps were scattered about and a rough bed stood in the corner. Mice crawled throughout the structure. In the kitchen there was dried blood on the sink and a few knives of various shapes and sizes. A few half burned candles were strewn about.

Outside, there was a fire pit with a cooking spit for roasting meat. There were bones scattered in the bottom of the fire pit. Off to one side were two sawed off waist high stumps with pieces of leather attached to them. Jack picked up one of the pieces of leather nailed to the stump. "Not sure what this might be. Don't bird trainers tie the legs of the birds to hold them?"

Shelly took a closer look at the fire pit. "Jack, take a look at this. What kind of bones do you think these are?"

Jacked moved the large bone with a knuckled end using a stick. "They might be human. I am no expert, but I have seen plenty of deer bones in the woods before and they don't look like that one. It's too short for one thing". He pointed at a large bone resembling a human femur. It appeared to be about sixteen inches long.

As they moved around the cabin they saw two heavy wooden cellar doors built off the back of the structure. A large rusty metal bar was jammed between the metal door handles. They were tangled with overgrown raspberry vines which made them difficult to open.

Jack holstered his gun and used both hands to pry open the cellar door against the impeding vine growth. The doors were thick and heavy, made of what appeared to be about two inch hand hewn lumber planks.

Half log steps led down to what appeared to be a dark fruit cellar. Jack pulled out his flashlight and illuminated the stairs. Drawing his gun he started down the steps. Shelly stayed on top and kept an eye on the surrounding woods in case anyone was nearby.

As he descended the steps, a disgusting smell of rotting flesh nearly overwhelmed him. When he got to the bottom of the stairs, he realized this was not a fruit cellar.

There was a wooden post sunk into the dirt floor with handcuffs hanging from it. Shining the light around the approximately twelve by twelve foot room, he stopped on a pile of bones in the corner. There were two human skulls atop the heap. This was a dungeon of sorts. In another corner was the source of the smell. A partially decomposed body lay on the floor.

"Shelly, this is it. We have bodies down here!"

Jack returned up the steps. "Go ahead take a quick peak. It is safe. We need to get out of here fast though and stake this place out. We want to make it look like we have never been here if we can."

Shelly viewed the evidence quickly and returned up the steps visibly shaken. "My god, those poor people who died in that rat infested hole in the ground."

Jack closed the door on the shed and replaced the metal bar in the door handles. Lastly, he threw the broken tangled raspberry vines over the door again to conceal them.

"This has got to be our guy for sure. I hope he still uses this place."

Jack set up another camera in the woods and they started back towards the trail. As he tied the camera to a tree branch he noticed pine boughs carefully placed on a trail to the rear of the shack. Walking over to the spot, he slowly removed a branch revealing a pit with sharpened wooden stakes at the bottom of it. He called Shelly over so she could see it.

"He has booby traps set up. We need to be really careful getting out of here. Watch your step and be observant. This looks like something right out of Vietnam. Sheriff Campbell will be interested in this I bet. This would be the place to start with his dogs."

As they walked back toward the boat landing they could see two birds now circling them overhead. Another grouse flushed off the trail startling the jumpy couple.

"That is just great." responded Shelly as she dropped to one knee, revolver drawn and pointed at the sound of the escaping bird. "This whole thing gives me the creeps."

"That is actually a good sign he is probably not around. He would have flushed it instead of you."

As they walked Jack continued to speak softly.

"We will get some extra people to stake this place out undercover. It kind of looked like he had not been there for awhile."

Shelly responded,"What about those bodies? We need to report that and get this worked over as a crime scene."

Jack looked at her and shook his head.

"Once that happens, this guy will probably never return if he sees a bunch of FBI activity. Let's just wait a day or two and see if we can nail him on our own."

The long walk back to the landing seemed somewhat uneasy knowing this manic could be lurking in the bushes along the trail. The booby trap they had uncovered was also a bit unsettling. A big buck deer spooked from his bed flashing a big whitetail. They both jumped with guns drawn as the big animal bounded through the woods. Jack smiled at Shelly as she put her hand over her heart.

"Kind of reminds me of my FBI training. You know, where the good guy and bad guy targets pop up on the shooting course. We use game animals for the good guys up here. They tend to surprise you more than those damn wooden targets."

When they got to the landing a fisherman was launching a fishing boat. Jack spoke with the man and said they were working for the Department of Natural Resources.

He explained they were taking creel reports and checking on the condition and usage of the landing.

"Howdy, how has the fishing been?"

"I have done okay so far this year," the man replied.

"How often do you use this public boat landing when fishing Tanner's Lake?"

The man pushed his cap up and responded.

"Well, this is the closest landing to my house, so I'm probably up here at least once a week during the summer fishing season."

Jack wrote his answer in a notepad and asked the next two questions.

"Is the landing ever too crowded when launching your boat? Do you think there are enough parking spaces?"

"Usually I am the only one here. Sometimes around the opening weekend you will see a few guys. This old blue truck is usually parked here."

"We are also curious about that truck as we are trying to locate the owner. We think he might park it here all the time which is illegal. Have you ever seen anyone driving it when you're here?"

"One time I saw a big dude unloading a canoe off it. He carried it over to the dock and started paddling up that way."

The man pointed to the north.

"Did he say anything to you?"

"No, he wasn't a friendly guy at all. I said hello and he just sort of grunted and kept walking. He had greasy long hair and looked like he had been in the woods for awhile."

"What do you mean?"

"I don't know. He just had ragged camouflaged pants and a buckskin looking shirt of some kind. I guess just the sheer size and long greasy hair with a long messy beard made him look like an original mountain man from the eighteen hundreds or something. He was really big, too. Like a pro basketball or football player's size."

"Anything else you can describe about him?

"Not really, except he did have a big mean dog that barked at me until he called it off."

"About how long ago did you see this guy?"

He pondered the question for a moment. "It would have been two weeks ago Wednesday. That was the last time I was up here."

"Okay, well that's about it. Thanks for the information. If we see him we are going to remind him there is no overnight camping in the state forest except in official campgrounds."

The fisherman nodded. "No problem. I hope you are not going to close this boat launch." Jack shook his head. "Not to worry about that. It is the only public landing on this side of the lake. We just want to make sure it is not getting too much use. They are considering building another one about twenty miles further south. The DNR just wants to do a little survey work and see if it is even needed. No sense wasting money building a boat ramp if this one is sufficient."

As they drove off in their boat Shelly shook her head and slapped his leg with the back of her hand.

"Well, aren't you just the good old boy DNR guy slinging the bullshit. You are lucky he didn't ask for your badge."

Jack just smiled at her. "He was probably just glad I didn't ask for his fishing license."

Shelly looked at him. "So what is next super sleuth?"

"I say we go up and place a few cameras around that canoe and see what is going on just north of here. A big primitive looking dude with a canoe sounds like our man."

Shelly agreed but was hesitant. "It seems like we are getting really close to this guy. What if he doesn't go peacefully Jack? Maybe we should just call Sheriff Campbell and FBI reinforcements right now."

"He probably won't go peacefully. We are going to just have to do whatever it takes to get him cuffed. Hopefully we can take him alive. If we bring in a full blown FBI team somebody will probably get killed by this guy. What if he sets up as a sniper or something like Sheriff Campbell mentioned? Maybe we can avoid that if it is just the two of us. He may never know we're here until it's too late for him."

The boat slowly pulled into the reeds of Rice Bay as evening approached. The water was calm as Jack took a couple of casts toward the lily pads. His lure moved through the clear water with an enticing action. He wanted to look like a fisherman.

"This is about where I was when those birds attacked me. Maybe he is watching us right now for all we know. I kind of feel like we're the bait hanging out in this guy's turf. Keep your eyes open and your gun ready. He is definitely not the kind of enemy we want to be captured by."

They took their time and slowly pulled into the reeds about one hundred yards from where the canoe was hidden.

Jack looked at Shelly. "We are going to bushwhack it the rest of the way over to the canoe in case someone is watching. You will see what I mean by the woods being thick."

They slowly worked their way along the shoreline climbing over downed trees and thick aspen trees. Eventually they hit a small trail which they began to follow.

Another ruffed grouse exploded from the cover startling Shelly again. "Damn, I can't get used to those things."

Jack just smiled at her and kept moving forward with his shotgun pushing the small branches from his face. Jack turned and whispered at her.

"Someday I will take you grouse hunting. It's really fun. They keep you on your toes when a killer is lurking about, too. Of course that is not a concern when hunting normally."

She rolled her eyes at him and they continued onward through the thick canopy of trees. They moved slowly, pushing through the thick brush as if they were hunting.

Jack used a stalking tactic he often employed on whitetail deer. Walk about twenty steps and then stop for a full minute, observing. Then move another twenty feet and do the same thing. It took some time to cover ground with this method but they were not in a hurry. The last thing they wanted was to be heard from a distance by a crazy guy like Jepson. No doubt he would probably attack if he did hear them coming.

Moving slowly and listening was the key. Hopefully they would hear the Griffin first. A big man like that was bound to make some noise traveling through the thick woods.

15

The Griffin was almost ready to play cat and mouse with his latest victim. He stood over the staked down man explaining the rules of the game to him. Perched above him tethered on their stumps were the tame eagle and falcon. Lobo stood near the man's face licking his chops.

"The rules are quite simple my friend. I am going to let you go and give you a twenty minute head start. If you can make it off the reservation land you are a free man."

He continued on with his rambling, walking around the terrified man. "On the other hand, if we catch you, we are going to eat you for dinner."

With that he threw his long greasy hair backwards laughing at his frightened victim. "For my portion, I will make you into wood grilled barbecued skewers of meat. Doesn't that sound delicious?"

He paused, pondering the situation for a moment.

"Before we start, I am going to give you a little example of what I mean to keep you motivated. I do not want this hunt to be too easy. This should help remind you that you are literally running for your life."

He took fish from a bait bucket and smeared it over the man's feet and ankles. Then he brought over the tethered eagle.

The big eagle hopped on the man's leg with its sharp talons and ripped a piece of flesh with a single bite from its powerful beak. Blood flowed from the fisherman's wound as the Griffin picked up the eagle with his leather arm protector.

"Now you know what I mean by dinner. We also need a good blood trail to make it a fair chase. I will warn you that the surrounding woods are also booby trapped. For the most part the traps are designed to maim the victim, not kill. If we catch you, more than likely you will still be alive. We want to keep your meat fresh."

The man became angry and tugged at his restraints. The Griffin smiled and responded to his efforts.

"That's the spirit. Get angry. It will help your survival chances. I like your attitude. Being a sportsman, I am even going to give you a weapon."

He picked up a stout hickory pole and slapped it against his open hand. "This can make a fine club and much more if you become creative."

"I will warn you not to try and use the club on me after I cut your restraints. I will kill you slowly right here and now if you do."

With that he pulled a large knife from his strapped deer skin sheath and cut the man's bindings. The man sat up and cowered in fear as the Griffin stood over him. The Griffin dropped the hickory pole next to him and pulled a pocket watch from his camouflaged pants. Opening it he looked at the man quizzically. "You have already wasted ten seconds my friend. You now have only nineteen minutes and fifty seconds." He went over and stroked the head of his wolf dog Lobo.

"My advice to you would be to head downhill toward the lake. It may be harder for Lobo to find you once you hit the water. He is very good at tracking blood from wounded animals."

He smiled at the terrified man. "Just thought I would be nice and give you as much of a chance as humanly possible." With that he bellowed in laughter as the terrified man grabbed the hickory pole and scrambled away down the trail.

The Griffin petted his dog and smiled. "Well Lobo, the chase is on. This is the ultimate game animal for you. Be aware of the club. Man does not have teeth to fight back as you know. But a man with a club is a different matter."

The fisherman hobbled down the trail as fast as he could. He used the hickory pole as a crutch. Stopping for a moment he ripped his shirt in half. He tied a tight bandage around his gashed leg trying to stop the blood flow.

A hunter and fisherman himself, he had survival skills but only against nature's elements. Skills like surviving overnight in frigid temperature until a rescue team arrived. There was no rescue team this time.

He had never really thought about being the prey. He had tracked many wounded deer during the season by blood trail. He knew it was tough and slow going without snow. He also owned a bird dog and knew what a dog with a good nose was capable of doing. The dog would have no problem following him.

As he approached the lake at the trail head he thought about stripping down and swimming. He was a decent swimmer. He went out a few feet and splashed along the shore line. It was still spring and the water temperature was still pretty cold. His fishing graph had registered it at only fifty five degrees. With his loss of blood he knew he could not swim far without hypothermia setting in.

He would probably drown if he tried to get away swimming. He would swim only as a last resort if that big bastard was coming after him, he thought. If he swims after me I could try to drown him.

Maybe I could take him under with me if I am going to die. Better to drown myself than be a torture victim of that lunatic. He knew the public boat landing was about five miles south. He decided to follow the shoreline south in shallow water to throw the dog off. He wondered if the mad man would honor the twenty minutes he was given. It must be getting close he thought.

As he frantically splashed along the shore he saw the eagle perched in a dying pine tree above him. He wondered if it was the same bird that had bitten him. Maybe they had already started after him.

The bird watched the man run the shoreline. As he got farther away the bird left its perch and took up another perch about a hundred yards south of the man. Looking at the bird as he approached the second time, he wondered if it was somehow identifying his location for the Griffin.

The Griffin had released the tethers of his pet eagle a few minutes early. Looking at his stop watch he smiled and released his dog. They both started down the trail. The Griffin carried a compound bow equipped with a quiver of arrows. The late evening sunshine glinted off the razor sharp broad head tips.

The dog picked up the trail immediately and followed it to the water's edge. He sat at the water's edge and waited for his master. The Griffin walked down the trail slowly taking close examination of his surroundings. Hunting a man was different he thought. It was fun knowing they were smarter than the other animals. Weak and slow but very smart, he pondered. "We will see how smart this fellow is," he said to his dog.

As he approached the water's edge, Lobo sat at the water where the trail ended. "He is taking my advice and following the water, Lobo. Now we need to find out which way he is headed."

With that the Griffin let out a loud blood curdling shriek. Hearing the call, the big bird took his eyes off the running man and took to the sky. The bird began to make wide high circles over the lake parallel to the man's location.

It did not take the Griffin long to spot his bird circling down the shoreline. He pulled a dead mouse from his vest pocket and held it up. Shrieking again the bird approached him and dove in for the mouse. The Griffin threw it up in the air as the eagle approached and the bird snatched it in mid air.

He smiled in approval as his training paid off. The bird flew back toward the scrambling fisherman, identifying his location.

"He is heading south, Lobo."

He gave the dog a waving arm command and the dog started running down the shoreline with nose to the ground. He shouted the word "HOLD" as the dog ran away. He had trained the canine to hold its victim similar to a police dog with a captive criminal. This was the dog's first real blind chase where his master was not right there when it was time to attack. Lobo knew the command "HOLD" well. Usually the command, "KILL" followed it shortly after in the past. That was the command he really excelled in.

The dog ran in excitement like a bird dog on scent periodically circling into the woods to find the trail. The Griffin trotted after his dog picking up the pace in an attempt to close in on his prey. Farther down the lake the man returned to the shoreline as it was faster to walk in the water.

Crossing the rocky shoreline he spotted a sharp jagged piece of broken granite about the size of his fist. Picking it up he intended to use it as a crude knife. It had a sharp point which was capable of doing some damage.

Hobbling along the rocky lake bottom made his progress difficult by water. On occasion a slippery rock would make him fall. He felt he had been on the run at least a good hour at this point. The Griffin must be coming by now. He noticed the eagle in a perch again not far from his location.

Suddenly he heard something approaching. He scanned his surroundings frantically expecting the worst. Noticing a very large wind blown pine tree he moved toward it. The trunk was nearly parallel to the water's surface and jutted out over the lake about twenty feet.

The dog came at him from behind like a bullet through the thick trees. It hit him in the back right shoulder and he fell to the base of the tree. The snarling growl of the vicious animal rang in his ear as he hit the forest floor. Lifting his left arm in protection the dog grabbed his arm in its mouth clamping down forcefully. As he struggled the dog increased the pressure.

The experience felt almost surreal to him as he struggled. There was no pain even though he was about to get torn to shreds by a wild animal. Seconds seemed like minutes as the life and death struggle of man and beast ensued. He had momentarily dropped his pole when he was hit from behind. He still had the rock in his right hand.

Swinging wildly he jabbed the dog in the left ear with the sharp rock. The dog shrieked at impact and momentarily released his grip. Lobo had never had a man fight back in the past. They had always been tethered or his master had been present.

Grabbing his pole the man seized the opportunity and struck the dog hard against its head while still on his back. This gained him another second to rise to his knee for a second blow. He grabbed the stout pole in the middle and used both sides to keep the dog off him like a karate expert.

The animal backed off for a second, barking and snarling at his unusual predicament facing this resourceful human. The man was now fully erect and screaming back at the dog. Blood streamed from his severely injured left arm but adrenaline had taken over.

He swung the pole back and forth at the dog and started moving out over the tree. The confused snarling animal followed out after him a few feet and stopped. The man tried to coax the dog out after him. "Come on you son of a bitch. You want to go for a swim pooch?"

He poked the pole in the dog's face, antagonizing it. The aggressive dog followed the pole out a few feet farther on the tree trunk. Going crazy the dog snarled at the man, ferociously snapping at the jabbing pole. Soon they were out ten feet or better over the water's edge. Glancing down, the clear water appeared to be about five feet deep.

Thrusting the pole into the dog's muzzle, he let the animal bite down on the pole. Instantly, they were in a tug of war scenario on the two foot wide tree trunk. With the dog firmly engaged, the man swung the pole to his right sending the animal airborne. He almost lost his own balance as the dog refused to let go. With one hand on the pole he went with the dog and dropped down and straddled the tree trunk.

When Lobo hit the water, he instantly released the pole and went under with a big splash. As he came to the surface the man jammed the pole into his head sending the dog under water again. This time Lobo surfaced out of range of the pole and swam to shore. The man considered jumping on him in an attempt to drown the dog but did not act soon enough. Lobo reached the shoreline and shook his coat in shock at the tenacity of this human.

This time the dog decided to wait for his master. He sat at the base of the tree and barked constantly at his treed prey. His master would make the kill when he arrived.

The man knew he could not stay in this predicament for long. The Griffin would be following his dog for sure. It did not seem feasible to try and fight this dog anymore. His left arm appeared to be torn up pretty good but his survival instinct had taken over.

Scanning the shoreline, a peninsula jutted out to the southwest about a mile down the shore. He could swim to the point, avoiding the dog and possibly gain some ground. It was probably a mile by water and three miles by shoreline to the point from his position. If the dog followed after him, he would attempt to drown it.

His mind raced with his options as he nervously gazed into the trees, fearful the Griffin would be emerging at any second. Hobbling to the end of the tree he jumped in about twenty feet out. The water was over his head.

As he jumped, Lobo moved out on the tree trunk. Afraid to leap after him, the animal barked wildly. He turned and floated on his back kicking away from the barking dog.

"That's it, stay there you stupid mutt. Just keep barking on that tree." As he kicked out further into the bay, the dog continued to watch him and bark madly from the tree. The cold water bit into him as the immediate danger from the dog subsided. Fortunately, the wind was with him and he floated with the waves toward the distant point.

The Griffin walked the shoreline smiling as he heard Lobo's excited yelps. He had heard the sharp yelp earlier but figured his dog must have been victorious in the struggle. He has him treed now he thought.

We will have to play this game more often, he pondered. Hopefully Lobo has not already killed him. He did not want to carry the man back to camp.

As the Griffin busted his way through the brush, Lobo's barking became louder. Finally his large frame emerged through the bush to his barking dog. The dog's ear was cut in half and dangling from the blow with the rock. The Griffin briefly looked at the wounded animal and became angry at his prey. "I will stitch you up at camp, Lobo," he said.

Accessing the situation he saw the man swimming a half mile out by now and heading for the point. "We must slow him down Lobo and get to the point before he does."

It was about three miles around to the point and he was halfway there by water. "You must keep him in the water for me Lobo. He can't last forever out there. We will not let him escape."

His eagle circled the bay and the Griffin called him closer. With a down sweeping arm command the bird dove at the swimming man, coming within feet of his head. The bird continued harassing dives and grazed the swimming man's chest on the second attempt. He saw blood flow from the two deep scratches inflicted by the eagles dive.

On the third dive, he was ready and used his pole to strike the bird while floating on his back. As it dove in, he struck a wing, injuring the animal. The eagle flew off like a wounded duck flying in an abnormal awkward fashion.

The Griffin was now in a full run on a deer trail which led to the point. He new the land well and had hunted the trail many times. Lobo ran ahead on the trail as if he knew where it led as well. The sun was beginning to set as the shadows crossed the trail's path.

The shoreline was now within reach as he approached the point. The frigid water was taking its toll and the injured man struggled to keep his head above the waves. When he was about thirty yards from shore, the weed line and lily pads made him struggle even more.

Battling his way through the weeds, the exhausted, weakened man reached the shore where he could finally touch bottom. Wading up through the water he collapsed momentarily resting on the shoreline. He hoped they were no longer pursuing him.

From his earlier effort walking the shoreline, he knew it would be tough to follow him. There were many obstacles and blown down trees which would make the distance to the point considerably longer.

Regaining his composure he began to follow an animal trail inland which headed south. It would be dark in about an hour. This might help him, he thought. As he worked his way south along the trail his condition deteriorated. His cold shaking body was slowing down even though he was telling his legs to move. He feared he might pass out and awaken to the Griffin standing over him. He must stay awake and keep moving. Finally his exposure to the elements and blood loss took over. He sat against a rock and rested, listening intently.

He heard a noise approaching from the south. He was prepared to meet his maker. He wondered if he should have just kept swimming until he had drowned. His best scenario would be to have the dog put him out of his misery quickly. He feared still being alive with the Griffin. He would make the dog kill him, he thought.

As the sound approached a man and woman suddenly appeared from the woods. It was not the Griffin. They appeared as angels to him. Who were these people in the woods?

McCabe had heard something on the trail and did not expect to see an injured man. Obviously in bad shape, Jack immediately went to the man and assisted. Taking off his coat he put it over the man. Shelly removed her coat and covered his legs. He was shaking and near delirious, obviously suffering from hypothermia. McCabe instructed Shelly, "We have to warm this guy up right now. Lie next to him and try to warm him while I build a fire. He could die before we get him out of here. Wrap your arms and legs around him. Your body warmth will help."

Jack picked a sheltered spot near a large granite boulder and started piling up small tinder and sticks. He took his knife and ripped a large piece off the lower portion of his tee shirt. Shelly huddled with her arms around the man trying to keep him conscious.

Jack looked at Shelly, "Cotton burns like gas when it ignites."

Holding a lighter to the strip of cotton it burst into flame and he placed it into the dry tinder. Almost instantly the dry wood caught fire and he continued to build upon it.

The fire grew in size as Jack added more dry wood and the man started to respond from its warmth. "We need to get him out of those wet clothes," said Jack.

They undressed the man and covered him with their own outerwear. Shelly removed her sweatshirt and put it on him. Jack zipped his coat around his lower body to keep in the heat.

He spoke softly to Shelly. "Stay alert and keep a look out, we might be in the Griffin's woods. I need to get more wood to stoke up this fire. It is going to be dark in about a half hour."

Jack left the immediate area looking for something to burn. Shelly huddled next to the man and he started to speak incoherently. One of his scrambled words was the Griffin. Shelly drew her revolver and sat near the man, peering into the darkening woods. Talking to herself, she was anxious for Jack's return.

"Come on Jack. Get back here. Where the hell are you?"

It had only been about ten minutes but it seemed like hours. She could almost sense the Griffin and his dog as they approached. Shelly stood up as she heard something up the trail. She expected Jack with an armload of wood. Sure enough it was her man emerging with a load of dry wood.

"I was hoping we could camp for a night. Unfortunately, just not under these circumstances. Three is a crowd, you know?" He beefed up the fire and went for more. "There is more where I just got his. I will be back in ten minutes. Keep your eyes open."

"No shit Jack. Maybe you should do the same." Shelly wondered if it wasn't a better idea to try to get him back to their boat right now. Spending a night out here was going to be risky with no backup. She didn't like the current situation one bit.

The Griffin heard them talking in the night air. They were close, maybe a hundred yards up the trail. Who are they? He wondered if it might be the Indian man. This is my domain. These are my woods. They are intruders. He slowed his pace and approached silently with his dog at heel.

He drew an arrow from his quiver, placing it on the bow string ready to shoot. As he approached, with the flicker of the firelight through the woods, he could see his prey. The fire illuminated the fisherman and someone else. He drew the arrow and aimed at the man he had been chasing. The instant he released the arrow he issued the "KILL" command to Lobo. The dog responded in a flash of fur and teeth.

The broad head arrow struck the man in the chest right next to Shelly. She turned to see the arrow go completely through the man and strike the boulder he was sitting against. At the same moment Lobo was on Shelly in a split second. She fired a shot into the air but was knocked off her feet. The speed of the canine was incredible.

It bit down hard on her left calf as she smashed its head with the butt end of her revolver. The dog released its grip and disappeared before she could get another shot off.

Springing to her feet, Shelly quickly checked the man for a pulse while looking for cover. He was already dead with an arrow through his heart. Fearing another arrow, she moved away from the fire into the darkness of the woods.

She was not in her element in these northern woods. The dog rushed her again biting her gun arm this time, causing her to drop the weapon. She instinctively pulled her stiletto and stabbed the dog in the side. The dog shrieked and released its grip, retreating into the woods. Picking up her gun she crashed through the brush wildly to get away. She ran for about ten minutes on her injured leg and stopped. A gun shot rang out in the night. It must be Jack, she thought.

McCabe had returned to the fire and saw the dead man with the arrow in his chest. As he checked his pulse to see if he was alive, a second arrow defected off a branch and stuck in a tree six inches from McCabe's head.

He fired a shot into the woods and hunkered down behind a nearby boulder. The Griffin smiled at their fear and went motionless. There was no moon. The woods were black at this point. You could not see your hand in front of your face.

The Griffin sat down with his dog fifty yards from the fire and watched McCabe. If he falls asleep I will send in Lobo, he thought. He wished he had brought his carbine. He could not get a good arrow shot with McCabe behind the boulder.

After a few minutes Jack knew he could not stay in the firelight. He would be a sitting duck. He slowly disappeared into the blackness of the forest and headed for what he believed was south.

It was time to get reinforcements he thought. He worried about Shelly's fate but thought she might be doing the same thing. He hoped she was still alive. It would be impossible to make an accurate arrow shot in the pitch black. She must still be alive and on the move like him. He had heard the snarling dog. He was not sure what that was about. He heard it shriek in pain, too. That was a good sign, he thought. Maybe she had killed it.

The Griffin watched McCabe exit and heard him wandering away through the brush. After an hour he moved in and claimed his prize as the small fire was now barely visible. He pulled his arrow out the man's back and put it in his quiver. Hoisting the dead man on his shoulder, he started back to camp up the deer trail. "Go home Lobo".

The Griffin followed his limping bleeding dog up the black trail. The dog did not need eyes to stay on the trail. It could scent its way back.

"We will eat this man tomorrow and hunt the two intruders at daylight. They will not get far. When we get back to camp we will return with my rifle."

Shelly tried to move toward the last sounds she had heard, but became hopelessly lost in the jungle blackness. She remembered what Jack had said. Just stay where you are and hunker down for the night against a tree and wait for light. If you move around you could fall off a cliff and get killed.

It seemed like sound advice, as she could not see a thing. She had a pen light but feared it would reveal her position to the Griffin if he was still around. We will get this guy now that we know he is here. We can hunt him down with a military team trained for combat in the woods. She wondered about Jack's fate and prayed he was safe. The cold night air made her shake as she had given up her sweat shirt and coat to the injured man. Eventually her eyes became accustomed to the dark and she could tell she was in a cluster of spruce trees. She lay on the ground under a large spruce snapping off the low hanging pine bows and using them like a blanket. She tried to remember some of the survival tips Jack had told her about.

As the Griffin neared his encampment he dropped his dead victim by the trailhead near his camp. The sun was starting to rise through the trees. The early dawn light provided enough light to reach camp quickly. He loaded his lever action rifle and headed back down the trail toward the lake.

The morning light had put Jack on the move as well. He needed to look for Shelly. The morning dew left everything soaking wet and cold. He knew she was in a tee shirt and bullet proof vest the last time he saw her. She was probably freezing if she was alive. The morning air temperature was about forty degrees. He hoped she had made some kind of shelter to last through the night and keep the dew off. He was very cold himself and needed to get moving.

When he returned to their campfire, the dead man was gone and there was no sign of Shelly. He found his shotgun still leaning against a tree and picked it up. The Griffin must not have seen it in the dark. He looked for where Shelly might have gone but could not see any sign of her. The morning dew had washed away any blood trail. He called out her name several times with no response.

His call fell on deaf ears as Shelly had momentarily passed out. She groaned as her left calf was swollen from the dog bite. She faintly cried out but Jack was too far away to hear by now. She closed her eyes and lay motionless again.

Jack moved up the same deer trail as the Griffin looking for Shelly. Maybe she was captured, he thought. In the mud he saw dog and human footprints along the trail. He followed the trail with his twelve gauge shotgun pointing up the trail and ready.

Before long he was near the edge of Rice Bay. Passing the canoe he sensed the Griffin was close. He could feel it. He heard a noise approaching from the north. Maybe it was a deer or possibly a man. It was hard to tell. It was something big coming his way.

Any noise traveled amazingly well in the cold morning air. This was not a squirrel, as noisy as they could sometimes be. It was a large animal with a steady pace. Not like a cautious whitetail working its way down a trail. Too noisy, he thought. It grew louder as it came closer and closer. It must be the Griffin. McCabe stood ready, hidden behind a pine tree. His mind raced wondering what he should try to do if Shelly was with him.

As daylight broke in the eastern sky, Shelly Montgomery awoke cold and shivering. She had blacked out momentarily but was not sure how long it had been. Her first thought was she escaped the attack and must find Jack.

A morning fog in the woods left her damp and cold. The thick covering of spruce boughs had kept her relatively dry. She assessed her condition. Her left leg was bruised and swollen from the initial bite. Her left arm was also bad but did not appear as severe. She did not know what happened to Jack. He was looking for wood when all hell broke loose. She had heard a gun shot probably fired by Jack. Maybe he got him, she thought.

Checking her leg again, it was severely gashed and swollen from the dog attack on her lower calf. The crushing force of the bite had left an ugly bruise with puncture wounds from the teeth. She had no sense of direction other than the faint light in the eastern sky emerging through the trees. She was not sure which direction she had run in the night.

The lake must be to the west, she thought. As she stood up, pain coursed through her bleeding lower leg. It was extremely sore and she limped badly when putting weight on the leg. She began moving cautiously through the woods with her revolver drawn. Eventually she located the camp site from the night before. The lake was about fifty yards to the west of the camp. The fire still smoldered with charred logs.

No sign of Jack or the dead man with the arrow in his heart. Whoever killed him must have taken him, unless Jack had carried him out. There was a deer trail with footprints heading north. The shot from the arrow had come from that direction as well. It seemed to be the logical course of action to follow the trail north.

Maybe Jack had been captured by the Griffin, or possibly he is going after him. She hobbled up the trail toward the stashed canoe. She could not wait for reinforcements. Jack could die before help arrived if the Griffin had him. She was uncertain how to proceed, but her instinct told her to follow the trail at least for a little while.

She could go back to their boat if nothing turned up and get help. Shelly feared the worst, as she knew Jack would be looking for her. He must be around here somewhere, if he is still alive.

16

The sun light rose over the trees as ducks flew into Rice Bay. The approaching noise sounded like it was now right around the bend in the trail.

McCabe felt his best bet to locate Shelly and the Griffin was to wait at the bottom of the trail by the canoe. He would be back for it soon, he thought. He would probably try to leave the area by water after last night's encounter.

Or, Shelly might make her way back down the trail if she was still alive. He waited and listened intently. McCabe sat motionless hidden in the pine tree. The steady sound of footsteps grew louder and louder. The figure of a large man suddenly appeared making his way down the trail through the thick brush.

It was indeed Mr. Jepson, AKA "The Griffin", carrying his latest victim over his shoulder. Apparently he intended to take his human prize with him in the canoe.

He was dressed in buckskin and looked like an animal himself. Bearded and bloody, he grunted as he moved down the trail with his load.

As he approached the trail head, McCabe stood up pointing the shotgun at him and ordering him to freeze. In a single motion, Jepson wheeled around with the man on his shoulder. A rifle from under his deer hide poncho cracked as the bullet whizzed past McCabe. Obviously he was not intending to be taken peacefully.

Simultaneously, McCabe squeezed his own trigger and sent a load of twelve gauge buck shot at the large man's upper torso. Most of the pellets tore into the dead body draped over his shoulder.

The Griffin dropped the corpse and fired two more rounds as he retreated up the trail, disappearing around the corner. While he ran up the trail, McCabe pumped the shotgun and returned another round through the brush at the retreating man. He could hear him moving up the trail as he began to pursue.

The body which he had discarded lied motionless on the trail. McCabe checked for a pulse and got none. It was the man they were helping last night. He turned the man over and saw the arrow wound in his chest. His bowels were removed as if he were a gutted deer. He was obviously dead prior to his shot. McCabe chased the hulking man up the trail firing another load of buckshot as he saw a brief glimpse of him disappearing into the hillside. The Griffin returned fire, slowing McCabe's pursuit.

He appeared to be hit, as blood lined the trail. But some of the blood was probably from the gutted man at the bottom of the hill. It was hard to tell how bad he was hit. It looked as if he was limping in the brief glimpse McCabe had of him.

As McCabe cautiously approached, he could see a fresh blood trail along the ledge of the cliff. Adrenaline flowed as he slowly walked out toward where he last saw the man. As he rounded the corner, a large snarling dog lunged at him from a boulder above.

Instinctively, McCabe fired, hitting the dog in the chest. The animal shrieked in pain and hit him in the upper left shoulder on his fall. The dog's momentum knocked McCabe off the small ledge and he fell about eight feet through the sumac brush to a boulder below.

He dropped his shotgun as he fell and his right leg was wedged between two large boulders. Pain shot up his leg and he feared it was broken. The dog lay dead at the bottom of the cliff ten feet below him.

He remained motionless for a few minutes listening. Pulling his nine millimeter automatic from his vest holster he remained frozen. Above him he could hear the shuffling of feet. Blood dripped through the brush near his position.

He thinks I am dead from the fall, thought McCabe.

He heard the man circling behind him on another trail leading downward. A horrific scream pierced his ears as the Griffin let out a shrill cry. Two hawks began circling above McCabe's position shortly after the scream. Desperately, he tried to free his right leg from between the rocks.

He grimaced in pain as he could see a piece of bone piercing the calf of his leg. He knew he had a compound fracture and was in serious condition. Suddenly, from above his position, a heavy woven fish net was tossed upon him.

He struggled in the net and fired two shots above. Minutes later he heard footsteps below his location. Suddenly, the net was drawn closed and pulled down with such force that it pinned McCabe to the rock.

The Griffin tied off the net's draw rope to a tree and began climbing the boulder to retrieve his trapped prize. He had used the net on deer before. This was the first time he had ever trapped a human in it. He was proud of himself.

As he reached the top of the boulder, McCabe managed to fire his revolver while the net pinned him to the rock. The bullet hit the large man in the shoulder as he was rising over the boulder.

He moved to the side and McCabe could not change the direction of his gun.

The large man climbed on top of McCabe, hitting him about the head. McCabe fired another round in the struggle but missed. The bullet ricocheted off the boulder next to him.

Soon the Griffin had his arm pinned and slammed his hand against the rock. McCabe's hand went numb from the pounding and he lost his grip on the weapon. The revolver fell to the ground below. He could barely move with his leg wedged between the rocks and the heavy fish net pressing him tight to the boulder.

The Griffin sat back, laughing at his trapped animal. He bellowed a loud laugh as blood bubbled from his shoulder wound. It did not seem to bother him very much.

"You are very good my friend. Not many have bloodied the Griffin in a battle." He pulled the net off McCabe when he saw his broken leg wedged between the boulders.

"This is very ironic for you to be tied to a boulder. That is the normally the role of Prometheus. Maybe the eagle will eat your liver tonight instead of mine."

McCabe sat up horrified, at the site of this beast. Scraggly dirty shoulder length black hair covered half his face. A full beard of bloody slime covered the rest of his face. His eyes gleamed like that of a wild animal. A necklace of human teeth draped his neck and chest.

The Griffin pulled a large knife from under his animal skin poncho and revealed it to McCabe. He poked him in the injured leg and laughed as McCabe screamed in pain.

"The Griffin was a doctor in the Civil War. I specialized in amputations. Maybe we should amputate your leg to free it from the boulder?"

He looked at McCabe in an inquisitive way, as if his answer would matter. He poked McCabe again with the knife for a reaction, cutting him above the calf.

McCabe tried to keep his composure and told the crazy man that would be a bad idea. "If you kill me there will be federal agents all over these hills looking for me."

The large man arched his back and laughed a loud bellowing guttural roar. He reached down with his knife and sliced a piece of meat off McCabe's leg and took a bite of it.

Then he held up the remaining morsel for his hawks. A bird swooped in and landed on his shoulder.

"Do you think I am worried about more federal agents, you fanatical foolish man? Do you really think you can instill fear in a man like me? I am the Griffin. I am not capable of fear." McCabe pressed his palm on the new wound in a feeble attempt to stop the bleeding.

"But you, my pathetic little man, are a different story. You will cringe in fear watching your flesh disappear as we keep you alive and slowly devour you."

He sliced another small piece of flesh from McCabe's leg and fed it to his bird. McCabe was near passing out and the large man slapped his face.

"You stay awake, my friend, and pay attention. We will eat you piece by piece. First your leg so you cannot run away. I will heat up my knife in the fire pit. We need to cauterize the wound so you stay alive. I believe in fresh meat off the bone. I don't keep a refrigerator you know."

He spoke to McCabe in a crazed nonsensical way as if he was truly a friend talking about food storage. As if McCabe should offer some opinion on the matter of how to store his own flesh.

"You have killed my beloved dog and best friend. You shall suffer by unimaginable methods for this crime." He climbed off the boulder and McCabe could see the smoke from a fire he had started. Far above him he could hear something moving.

Shelly Montgomery slowly hobbled up the trail toward the noise above. She had heard the gunfire earlier and then the horrific screams through the woods. Several of the shots sounded like a shotgun. She hoped they were from Jack's gun.

Her short walk up the trail had turned into a full day struggle on her bad leg.

She had been moving toward the sounds for several hours now. Her leg was badly damaged from the bite and did not look good. She was cold and damp from exposure to the elements.

As she moved closer to the noise of the camp, she tripped a sapling with wooden spikes that slammed into her arm from the side of the trail. One wooden spike went completely through the meat in her right forearm. Her gun fell to the ground as she briefly screamed from the pain.

The Griffin perked up his head as the knife was now red hot. He had heard the scream. He spoke to his bird softly. "Perhaps you should go see what we have caught in our traps."

Montgomery pulled off the wooden spike and ripped the bottom of her tee shirt, wrapping her arm in a make shift bandage. It did not appear to have severed an artery.

Picking up her gun with her left hand she continued to move up the trail. She could see the smoke from a fire through the tree tops. A large eagle perched in a tree at the cliff's edge. She continued moving along the rock ledge toward the cave.

Fear gripped her as she had seen her enemy briefly the night before. She had never been involved in the pursuit of anyone even close to the Griffin's capabilities in her FBI career.

They should not be here chasing this maniac alone, but it was too late to retreat. The moment was now and she must succeed. To fail would be to die a slow horrible death at the hands of a mad man.

The Griffin returned to the boulder with the knife gleaming red hot from the fire. McCabe looked up at him unable to move.

"I suppose you would like me to explain the procedure you are about to undergo. First, I will amputate with my smaller skinning knife," he said.

"Then, I will cauterize the wound with this big hot knife. That is my favorite part of the procedure. I am sure you will enjoy it as well."

He talked like a deranged doctor of sorts.

"I always like to explain the procedure to my patients. There is always a slight risk of infection with my surgeries. But I will burn the wound to reduce the risk. So are you in agreement with the surgery?"

The Griffin grabbed Jack's head hair, moving it up and down rapidly to indicate a yes. "Excellent, well lets get underway."

McCabe watched in horror as The Griffin sliced around his broken leg bone and freed the leg at the calf. Instantly he slapped the big hot knife to the wound and laughed.

McCabe screamed in pain as the red hot blade was pressed to the dangling flesh at the stump.

"I would have given you something to bite on. But I wanted to see what it might do to your teeth. You will be a fine addition to my necklace."

McCabe stiffened and grunted from the pain, nearly foaming at the mouth from the intensity of it all. His lungs shortened in breath and his body heaved from the intense pain.

The Griffin sliced the remaining tissue from the amputated extremity and pulled it from the rock. The Griffin held up the amputated foot and smiled at his surgical work.

"We will cook this on a rotating spit," he exclaimed to McCabe.

"You will have some nourishment yourself. I would like your opinion on my cooking ability," he said with a grin on his face.

Grabbing McCabe, he pulled him from the large granite boulder and down to the campfire burning below. Barely conscious, McCabe looked at him in horror as he cooked his foot on a spit over the fire.

"Tomorrow night for supper we will take your left arm," he explained to a fainting McCabe. He scorched his amputation again to wake him up. Please, you must stay awake my friend. I don't get much company in these parts." McCabe screamed as the hot knife was applied again.

The Griffin sawed a piece of cooked flesh from the foot and tossed it to McCabe. "Eat it. I want you to know how delicious your flesh tastes."

McCabe refused and the hot knife was applied to his wound again. He managed to hit the Griffin with a right cross and knocked him back a couple feet.

The Griffin smiled at him and removed a front tooth from the punch. “You knocked out a tooth. I will take your teeth one by one for that. I will take them while you are still alive.”

The Griffin pounced on the weakened McCabe and hit him several times with forceful blows to the face. McCabe was temporarily knocked unconscious from the attack.

Shelly Montgomery was slowly moving toward the screams. Now on the cave ledge they were directly below her. Darkness was beginning to fall on the camp and the fire cast shadows of the two men into the woods.

McCabe regained consciousness and awoke to the Griffin cooking his leg over the fire.

“Welcome back to the land of the living, my feisty friend. I will make you wish you were dead in good time.”

The Griffin turned McCabe’s lower right leg and foot on the roasting spit over the fire. The stench of his burning flesh sickened McCabe.

His hands were now bound with rawhide ties. He inconspicuously tried to loosen them when the Griffin was not looking. The Griffin sawed off a toe from the rotating meat spit and popped it into his mouth. He chewed it as if it was a delicacy.

He opened McCabe’s wallet and looked at his identification.

“You are cooking up well Mr. Jack McCabe. I bet you never thought you would go out to dinner with a friend and be the main course.”

He sliced off another chunk of leg meat and threw it to one of his hawks tethered on a stump near the fire. “Which toe would you like Jack? You will eat, even if I have to cram it down your ungrateful throat. We will be able to live off you all week. The big feast will come when you are dead. That’s when we will feast on your heart and liver.”

He sawed off another toe and waved it under McCabe’s nose.

"Smells good, doesn't it? Now open your mouth or I will smother you until you open it yourself."

McCabe struggled and turned his head as the man pressed the flesh to his lips. McCabe kicked and struggled as best he could as the Griffin covered his nose and mouth with his big hand.

"When you open your mouth to breath, you will swallow your toe."

McCabe gasped and the flesh entered his mouth choking him more. As he gagged on his own flesh, the Griffin stopped and laughed at him.

"That's it Jack. What do you think? Good?"

McCabe spit in disgust, blurting out expletives of every nature in anger at his tormenting captor.

"Maybe you should not speak at all Jack. Every time you open your big mouth you seem to put your foot in it." The Griffin laughed at his own humor and enjoyed McCabe's helpless position.

He hated cops and he would do a special job making this one suffer. In his pleasure, he had momentarily forgotten about Montgomery's scream from the booby trap.

Slowly limping down the ledge she could now see the big man sitting at the fire with McCabe slumped over to the side. She couldn't tell if Jack was alive or dead. The smell of burning flesh was apparent. She feared he was already dead.

The fire light flickered in the darkening forest around the camp. She saw a small opening between two pine trees and silently moved toward the gap. She could see the Griffin and waited for him to busy himself with the campfire.

As he stirred the fire, she popped out from between the spruce trees. Pointing the .45 caliber revolver with her good left hand, she approached on his backside.

"Freeze, on the ground now!" she screamed.

The crazed man just laughed and stood up. He turned to face her.

"Get on the ground, right now! Hands behind your head now! I swear I will blow your head off," screamed Shelly.

"So you have come to join us for dinner. How nice of you. Do you know Jack?" The Griffin did not fear women. He believed all women were weak and could not hurt him. He was used to Mexican women in his camp and dominating them. He wondered who this Mexican female might be. Maybe she was brought to his camp by the Indian man.

As he stood up he reached for his knife under his poncho. He began walking toward her. Montgomery triggered a round from her .45, hitting him directly in the chest. The large man flew backwards and landed on his back.

She hurried over to McCabe to check his vitals. As she was doing this a hawk flew into her face. She swung her pistol at the bird and Jepson suddenly lunged at her from his knees. A direct hit from the .45 slug had not completely dispatched him.

The wounded man grabbed the gun and slammed her arm into the fire, forcing her to drop it. Weakened but refusing to die, the Griffin's massive strength was still overwhelming.

McCabe kicked him with his good leg trying to get him off of her. As the struggle ensued, Montgomery reached to her lower calf retrieving her concealed knife.

She brought the stiletto up in one motion to his neck and pushed the release button. The blade pierced the gruesome man's neck, killing him almost instantly.

She pushed his limp body off her and watched him quiver in his last moment of life. It was over in an instant. She turned her attention to McCabe and hugged him, crying.

"Oh my god Jack your leg."

She made a crude tourniquet and applied it to his severed leg. Jack was going in and out of shock. He was not really aware of what had happened and was barely conscious. "I've got to get you out of here tonight Jack." She looked around as darkness fell on the woods.

She remembered McCabe's survival advice. "What would you do Jack?"

He groaned, barely conscious from the blood loss. He could not supply an audible answer. She knew she had to take action if he were to survive. She cut the animal skin off of Jepson's body and placed it over McCabe for warmth. Next she took some hot rocks from the fire pit and placed them under the skin blanket around him.

McCabe's foot and lower calf lay half roasted in the dirt from the struggle. She removed it from the area and threw it into the woods. There was no possible way to save the tissue. She didn't want him to see it if he woke up.

Next she checked Jepson to make sure he was dead. There was no pulse she could detect. Her knife still protruded from the side of his neck. She had hit him squarely in the chest with a round from her .45 caliber. He was dead. He lay on the ground face up, blood still oozing from his neck and chest wounds. It looked like Jack had hit him with some of his shots as well. His eyes were open and rolled back in his head. She stoked up the fire and made a crude torch from the animal skins the Griffin had left hanging in camp. Wrapping a sturdy stick with the fat side out from a deer hide, she made a torch.

Lighting the make-shift torch, she started down the hill toward the lake. She must find the canoe and get help tonight, she thought. Her cell phone was useless as there was no signal on this corner of the lake. The path was dimly illuminated from the crude torch as she made her way down to the lake.

"What other fucking animals does this asshole have," she said to herself as she hobbled down the trail. She grimaced in pain as her foot was swollen to nearly twice its normal size from the dog bite the night before. It had taken her all day to follow the trail and the gunshots she had heard. Walking on her leg was not doing it any good.

Both arms were also in poor condition. She had burned her left arm severely in the fire during the struggle with the Griffin. Her right arm had a bad puncture wound from the wooden stake and ached badly.

Soon she was at the marsh and the trail that led to the canoe. Their boat from the night before was too far away through the woods. She could not walk that far again. The trail darkened as the torch burned lower. She finally arrived at the canoe, and climbed in grabbing a paddle as her torch went out.

As she pushed off in the dark, she used her left armpit and injured right forearm in an attempt to paddle the craft. It was a feeble stroke but she was moving out of the reeds slowly. She cried softly as the boat moved through the weeds with her struggling efforts. She could see the distant lights of Flanagan's resort across the bay.

Luckily the wind was blowing from the northeast pushing her toward the resort. This is crazy she thought as she kneeled in the bottom of the canoe. She had learned that if you lower your center of gravity in a canoe it will not tip as easily. If she capsized, she would drown for sure in her condition. Without the wind at her back, this would be a hopeless crossing of the lake.

Struggling with her own pain, she started across the big bay with awkward paddles. Suddenly the lights from a night fisherman appeared in front of her. She screamed for help and a spotlight eventually lit up the canoe.

The boat cruised up to her slowly and the spotlight illuminated her bloodied body. It was George White Owl, the Indian man she had met at Flanagan's tavern the night before.

"Please help me. I am an FBI agent. We have an injured agent and a dead man in the woods."

First he did not say anything. He pulled up to the canoe and tied it to his boat. He shined his light on her pathetic unarmed condition and then he spoke.

"Tell me Miss FBI Agent. Why should I help you?"

"Do you think that crazy man conspired to do all this carnage on his own?"

"Where do you think all those bodies came from last winter? Do you know what I do for a living Miss FBI agent?"

Montgomery glared at him and pleaded that she needed medical assistance immediately for McCabe. She knew instantly that White Owl must be involved.

"We have an agent with a severed leg. He will die if we don't get him to a hospital soon."

"You already know I am an over the road trucker, primarily making runs from Minneapolis to south Texas. All the way to the Mexican border towns sometimes, like Laredo, El Paso and Brownsville."

"You get paid for the cargo you haul. Sometimes I would pick up lucrative human cargo as well. When my clients were finished with them, I would charge a disposal fee. Mr. Jepson was my hired disposal agent. He would actually work for free as he is a crazy man."

He went on with a boyish grin on his face.

"I delivered used Mexican illegal immigrants to him. After servicing my American business clients, I told them I was moving them north to good jobs in Minnesota. Resort jobs on the community lakes in the region. Most of them were very excited about it and looked forward to a new life."

She could see his involvement at this point and feared for her life. "We have our man. He is dead. I killed him. Nobody has to know about you. You could walk away from this whole thing. You have my word if you help me. You are not a suspect. You helped McCabe and showed him the reservation. We would not implicate you. We have no evidence."

White Owl smiled.

"I fed the Griffin human flesh from Mexico for the entire winter. I like Mexican girls. They are so gullible. Are you gullible Miss FBI Agent?"

Montgomery slid her hand around to her back side.

"If he wouldn't have started killing on his own, we would have been fine. He started feeding on tourists and fisherman. A total nut case as you surely know is true. I would take my trail workers up to his cave alive. We told them they first were to live in a nice little cabin and clear trails during the summer months for the forest service."

Montgomery had no weapons other than her throwing star in a small nylon case strapped to the small of her back. She was mad at herself for leaving her backup derringer in the rental boat.

"So why did you do it? Why did you kill all those poor people?"

White Owl smiled. "It was a pretty simple arrangement really. I bring him Mexican girls nobody cares about anymore. He gets rid of them for me so they can never talk about their slavery with my wealthy clients."

"Oh, and one more important thing I almost forgot. He paid me a great deal of money for the used girls. The Griffin is a rich man believe it or not."

He laughed and shook his head.

"He was just a crazy bastard who just wanted to be a hermit and have young girls. First he would use them for his sexual pleasure. After that he would use them for food. He became more obsessed with human flesh as time went on."

He continued, "He had lots of cash in his old cabin. He told me it was over one hundred thousand dollars in extortion money from his prison years."

White Owl continued.

"He terrorized many of his fellow inmates before arriving in Minnesota. They were afraid of him and gave him everything they had if he would not kill them. He got most of it from his rich little tourist boat buddy in San Antonio, who came from a wealthy family. Jepson used him big time."

Montgomery moved up the canoe closer to the tied bow of the fishing boat as he spoke.

"So it was all about money. What a waste of human life. My god, I pray for your soul. At least Jepson was insane. You are just a greedy horrible man to do such a thing."

"You are Mexican too. Just like those girls I brought to him from across the border. I am tempted to see if he is really dead. Maybe I could watch him dispose of you."

White Owl had difficulty believing he was really dead.

"He is a very hard man to kill. Fact of the matter, I am afraid of him too. I would not go into his camp in the nighttime. I met him with the Mexican girls on a trail head the 1st of every month. We met only at high noon when I could see his every move."

He paused, remembering the Griffin.

"One time I was alone and explained to him I couldn't get any girls. I thought he was going to kill me. He was upset and started throwing a psychotic tantrum. I was scared to death." He shook his head. "He was a crazy bastard alright. I never showed up empty-handed again."

He pulled a knife out of his belt and leaned over to cut the bow line to the canoe.

"I will hit your canoe going full tilt with my twenty five foot steel hulled boat and that will be the end of you, young lady. You will drown in this cold water if the collision doesn't kill you."

"It will be another boating accident with no navigational lights out in the pitch black of night. You should not be out canoeing in the dark without lights. It will be your fault and a tragic accident. Eventually they will find your dead friend at the Griffin's camp and understand why you were making such a risky night crossing in a canoe."

He mused at the thought.

"It seems kind of unfair to the Griffin when I think about it. To bad I can't feed you to him. He has acquired such a taste for fine Mexican girls. And you are a prime example for sure. He would have been pleased."

White Owl leaned over the bow with his knife to cut the canoe loose from his boat. Only four feet away from his head, Montgomery summed all her energy and threw the five sided steel star with her right hand.

The stiffness of her wounded forearm and her black belt training sent the spinning sphere hurtling at the back of his neck as he bent over to cut the rope.

The steel star struck him in the soft skin at the base of his skull on the back of his neck. He slumped over the bow of the big boat on impact. She quickly moved forward ready to fight but it was not necessary.

The throwing star gleamed in the boat's navigational lights revealing full penetration at the base of his neck. The remaining five stars glinted in the soft red and green bow light as the waves rocked the boat. The imbedded star had severed the brain stem. Montgomery climbed aboard his boat and cut the canoe free. White Owl was dead from the lethal blow.

"That is for all the girls, you bastard pig," she exclaimed as she climbed over his body into the boat. She turned the wheel toward Flanagan's lights and pushed down the throttle.

The boat rose up on the waves and sped to the resort. "Hang on Jack, I'm getting you help," she said to herself. She feared he might not make it. Noticing a marine band radio onboard she started calling mayday signals.

Almost instantly she had another boat on the radio and instructed them to call Sheriff Campbell. "Emergency situation, injured Federal agent. We need a chopper and medics to Flanagan's resort immediately.

Sheriff Campbell received the calls and dispatched all available staff. When Shelly arrived at Flanagan's docks there were already a chopper and several squads waiting. Sheriff Campbell met her at the dock and quickly assessed the situation.

"You need a medic right now," he said.

"No, I need to get you to Jack. He is in worse shape than me. He could die. It is right across the bay. Take the boat and have the chopper follow. Bring a stretcher. I'm okay."

The deputies removed White Owl from the boat and covered him on the dock. "Jesus", exclaimed the deputy as he covered the star sticking out the back of his neck.

The Sheriff jumped in the boat with Montgomery and two of his deputies and hit the throttle. The chopper stayed in communication and followed them across the lake.

The boat sped into Rice Bay and the location of the canoe they had spotted the day before from the air.

"This is it," shouted Montgomery as the spotlight scanned the shore. They trimmed up the outboard and moved into the beaver pond and the beginning of the marshy trail. That's it. Follow the trail up. There is a campfire burning up there. Jepson is dead. I killed him."

The men began moving up the hill, guns drawn, with strong flashlights illuminating the trail. Shelly struggled behind them, her wounded leg slowing the group.

"Go, go, it is right up the hill about two hundred yards," she urged. They moved on ahead of her.

The deputies moved up the trail quickly to the cave revealing the horrific scene. The fire light still flickered in the Griffin's face. He was propped up against a tree with the stiletto still sticking in the side of his neck. Eyes glassy, he was obviously dead.

McCabe was lying on the other side of the fire with a piece of rawhide around his neck. He had a large rock in his hand and was still clutching it. Two hawks sat on fireside stumps, tethered securely, watching the commotion.

"The deputy took McCabe's pulse. "He's still alive," he shouted.

The paramedics were right behind the Sheriff and within minutes had McCabe on a gurney and headed down the trail. The chopper landed in the Rice Bay lily pads with floats and awaited transport.

Shelly Montgomery stared at the crime scene and wondered. The Griffin was not propped up against the tree when she left. Nor did McCabe have a line around his neck. He must have fought him off, she thought in amazement. How could that be? He was dead.

Her thoughts turned to Jack. He was alive. Maybe he could tell her what happened someday. Her heart ached at his condition. She had fallen in love with him.

"Don't die on me Jack, she said, squeezing his hand as he went past on the medic's gurney. Another medical team put her on a gurney and followed after them. "Lie down agent Montgomery. We need to get you to a hospital right away, too".

The bay was illuminated with flashing boats and swarming with federal and local officials by the time McCabe and Montgomery were airlifted to Jackson Memorial Hospital.

Shelly Montgomery rode with Jack to the hospital. She wondered what this would do to her man. She worried he would be messed up from the psychological trauma. Most importantly, she hoped he would live to see another day.

She anguished over how he would handle the loss of his right leg. Within moments of their arrival a doctor pulled Shelly aside and explained that her own condition was serious.

Her leg was infected and her right forearm and left hand needed immediate treatment. Shelly Montgomery would have an extended stay at the hospital as well.

As the doctor sedated her with pain medication she drifted off to sleep thinking the last twenty four hours seemed like a surreal nightmare.

Shelly and Jack would both awake to the reality of what had transpired and it would change their lives forever.

17

Shelly awoke in the hospital first. Her left calf ached in pain as the nurse entered with her pain medication.

"You were in emergency surgery for your leg," she said.

"The doctor will be in shortly to explain it all to you. She handed her the medication. "Pain pills and antibiotics so you don't get infected worse."

Shelly smiled at the nurse and thanked her. "Is Jack okay? I need to know about Jack McCabe."

The nurse assured her. "He is alive. The doctor will be here soon to explain all the details. You just rest now until he gets here. I will tell the doctor you are awake."

The nurse checked Montgomery's vitals and then left the room

The doctor soon appeared through the doorway.

"Good morning Agent Montgomery. You are a lucky woman. You lost a lot of blood and your leg was severely infected from what appears to be an animal bite."

Montgomery sat up and spoke with a grimace of pain shooting from her lower leg. "It was a dog. A very big mean dog, I might add."

She paused and began to remember the night before. "Where is my partner? Jack McCabe, is he okay? Can I see him?"

The doctor paused. "He was in emergency surgery last week as well. He was very critical from blood loss. We gave him several transfusions and he is doing just fine."

A sigh of relief expelled from her lungs.

"Is he awake? What about his leg? Does he know what happened?"

The doctor explained.

"His leg was severed quite cleanly by a sharp knife. We really didn't have any problems with infection. He has been recovering for almost a week now and is doing quite well."

Montgomery looked at the doctor, confused. "What do you mean, a week?"

The doctor raised his eyebrows. "Shortly after you came in your body temperature rose to one hundred and five degrees. You were delirious for three days."

She nervously looked at the doctor. He continued on.

"Unfortunately, your lower calf was not cut with a sharp instrument, like your partner's. You experienced a ripping tearing wound that did not see treatment for approximately twenty four hours. Animal bites can be extremely infectious."

She cocked her head to listen better. "What are you trying to tell me?"

The doctor seemed very uncomfortable and blurted it out.

"In order to save your life we had to amputate your lower left leg." Montgomery threw up the sheet on her bed and looked in shock at her bandaged lower left stump.

"Oh my God," she exclaimed. "I can still feel my foot."

The doctor assured her that was normal and temporary. "The good news is the infection has finally stopped and the remaining portion of your leg is out of danger. We were afraid we might have to amputate above the knee if we could not stop the infection."

Anger momentarily set in. "Who gave you permission to amputate my leg?"

The doctor explained further.

"You were in danger of losing your life. Had we waited any longer you would have lost the leg from the hip down. We had to act immediately. Gangrene had already set into your foot and was moving up your leg. It would have eventually killed you left untreated."

The door opened and a familiar face entered in a wheel chair. It was Jack McCabe.

"I gave them permission partner. You were going to die if you kept the leg. You were out for three days and getting worse. I actually had the FBI contact your parents and got them to fly up for the official legal authorization. They are staying in Duluth."

Tears streamed down her face. "Jack! What did you do to me?"

He lifted up his right stump from the wheelchair. "Believe me when I say this. I know how you feel, Shelly. But we are alive. Just think of that right now."

The initial horror of losing her leg was a complete shock. She knew she should be happy she was just alive, but it was still difficult to accept the amputation. She looked at Jack and he seemed almost okay with his situation. She didn't understand how he could be so calm about it. As the afternoon went on, she realized he already had several days to accept his new body. He spoke to her about that and calmed her fears with some of the things the medical people had already told him. Things like the potential for a normal life with prosthesis and below the knee amputations. Jack didn't candy coat their new predicament.

"Life is not always fair Shelly, but it could be much worse. This is the shake we got, and we need to learn to live with it. If you want to be mad at someone, it should be me for putting you in the situation. I should have been more careful with this guy and got more people involved right away. I didn't think we would just run into him like we did."

Tears ran down Shelly's cheeks as she looked at Jack and realized he was right. An hour ago, her biggest fear on awakening in the hospital was Jack's condition. She was grateful he was alive and in some ways it seemed strange they were in basically the same condition. He was missing his right lower leg and she had lost her left lower leg. She brought that up to Jack and he broke the ice so to speak, discussing their new bodies. He nodded at her straight faced and told her he had pondered that point for almost two full days now.

Then he went on to explain that he expected them to be a force in one leg gunny sack races at the company picnic. His twisted theory had something to do with each of them having a good leg on the outside, provided they lined up that way. Or, if they chose, they could go with a good leg on the inside, and stumps on the outside, as another potential option by switching positions. She looked at him and first she got mad at his aloof attitude. Then as she thought about it she had to chuckle at his weirdness. He did not seem too much different from a personality perspective in terms of humor, than before the incident. He was still living life and cracking jokes. She thought he might be a basket case with untold post traumatic stress from his ordeal.

She looked at him closely. "Are you sure you are okay Jack?" He nodded and assured her he was fine. "I mean, is your head okay? You just had some maniac cut off your leg while you watched. Maybe it did something to you."

Jack acknowledged her concern. "The doctors, nurses and most recently, the psychiatrist have all been asking me the same question." Shelly cocked her head. "So what have you been telling them about it?"

Jack smiled. "I pretty much tell them I am glad to have survived the attack and it really pissed me off when he tried to cram one of my toes down my throat. Other than that, I explained to them that I always knew I could be in harm's way when I took on this job. Jepson was a total a nut and I am lucky to have survived. Without a great partner like you, I would have been dead for sure. You are going to get a medal for your heroic part in saving me and nailing the Griffin. What can I say? We were in war together and you came through for me. It's all okay with me because by all rights, I should be dead."

Shelly clutched his hand. "I am so happy you are alive. I thought you might not make it before I passed out. I love you Jack. I don't care about medals or any of that stuff. I did what I did because I was trying to save you. I couldn't give up. I know it hasn't been a long time but you mean everything…"

Jack squeezed her hand. "I love you too sweetheart, but you still need to get some rest. You just woke up from a three day coma about an hour ago. We have plenty of time to talk when you are stronger". The nurse entered and continued an intravenous feed to help Shelly gain strength. Her recovery progressed daily and she had plenty of time to think about what had happened.

As the days passed, Shelly began to accept her new body. There was much time for her and Jack to speak in between rehabilitation sessions. Days turned to weeks and as time went by they gave each other support. Eventually Jack even requested they be roommates in the hospital.

At times during the rehabilitation it even became comical. When Jack wasn't flirting with nurses he was making the most of his stay. He made a sign over their door called "Peg Legs" with the image of a Pirate. Sometimes he wore a black patch over his eye and acted like a pirate when he was bored. He insisted on being allowed a parrot in their room and Shelly thought he had gone off his rocker. Eventually she found the humor more entertaining than feeling sorry for herself. They were still in love and they both knew it.

However, when it came time to perform the real work involved with rehabilitation, they were both all business. They had been fitted with state of the art spring prosthesis legs funded by the

FBI. The prosthetic had a power foot that helped them walk and moved like a real ankle joint and foot. It had a computer built into it and was connected with nerve sensors at their stumps. They could actually train the computer to move the ankle and foot just by thinking. With practice, they worked hard to train the prosthetic computer and before long, both were walking again. With clothing on, you would have trouble knowing they were handicapped.

Unfortunately things had at least temporarily changed in their relationship. The reality was that the case was over and now they needed to learn how to adapt as disabled people on their own. They both needed some time apart to process what had transpired.

When the hospital discharged them they went their separate ways. Shelly returned to San Antonio to an office job with the FBI. She was considered a hero for her role in the Tanner's Lake case and received an award for her bravery and fortitude under extreme distress. She had lived up to her reputation as a top-notch tough agent in the bureau.

The FBI investigated White Owl's semi truck and found evidence of his involvement, based on Shelly's statements. Human hair samples and other DNA evidence match the victims found in Tanner's Lake. Trucking logs and a personal diary lead investigators to some of his clients who were purchasing his human cargo. Further indictments were soon to follow on these individuals.

She was also instrumental in putting Kyle Standish behind bars for his involvement in the River Walk murders. With statements from Standish, she took action to free the innocent man falsely imprisoned for the Griffin's hillside murder of his family. She took great interest in providing testimony and evidence from the case to get the victim who lost his family a new trial in the Texas criminal justice system. He was acquitted with her testimony on the Kyle Standish statement and now DNA evidence from the crime scene that matched the Griffin. Getting this man swift justice based on new evidence was extremely important to her.

She had met the man in prison a number of times and he was struggling to survive inside the walls. He was not a killer like many of the prisoners and some inmates took advantage of his weakness. When he was released it made her feel good that she could help him out of a terrible situation. He had been traumatized from the entire ordeal and would need ongoing victim support after his prison release. She personally got him into a free counseling program and got him his job back as a heavy equipment operator.

She was doing well in her new lifestyle but knew she did not feel right on a day to day basis. She missed Jack and wanted to see him. They spoke on the phone often about their new lives but that was not enough. She longed to see him in person.

Jack took his FBI disability agreement and started his own business in Minneapolis. He stayed in contact with Shelly and often tried to persuade her to go into business with him. Eventually, he convinced her to fly to Minnesota and visit him. He believed if she saw the business first hand, she would fall in love with it. They both knew they needed to be together. It was just a matter of time.

Finally, after closing the official book on the River Walk case, Shelly became bored with her new FBI desk investigator position. Because of her handicap, the FBI reassigned her from all field work as they felt it could affect her performance under fire. They said it was not discrimination but merely procedure. All field agents had to pass certain physical requirements which she could no longer meet. They were forced to reassign her within the agency. She was not happy with being strapped to a desk job so she accepted Jack's offer.

Shelly booked a flight to Minneapolis to visit him at his new business site. In his emails and on the phone, he had asked her if she wanted to become a partner in the new business venture if she fulfilled one condition.

He told her it was a restaurant bar on a popular Twin Cities lake. He called the place "Peg Leg's" and it had a large deck over-looking a first class marina on the lake. It had become a popular night club in the Twin Cities, currently bringing in a tidy sum of money. His clientele were mostly upscale wealthy boating enthusiast who lived on Lake Minnetonka. He told her she would be a celebrity owner and it was a constant party. He was known as Mr. Pete by his staff.

When the plane landed in Minneapolis, Shelly was escorted by a limousine to her new job site. The large white limo had a driver holding up a sign with the words "Shelly McCabe" at the main entrance.

As she approached the driver she questioned the sign.

"Is that supposed to say Shelly Montgomery by any chance? Did Jack McCabe hire you?"

The driver responded, "Yes he did Miss Montgomery. He said you would question the sign. He must know you quite well. Please climb in and I will transport you to your destination."

"And where might my destination be?"

"Mr. McCabe instructed me to just drive. I believe it is supposed to be some sort of surprise."

The limousine coursed along Lake Minnetonka with brief glimpses of the water. She had other ideas besides spending the remainder of her life as a one legged waitress in a place called Peg Legs. She looked at this whole trip as more of a rescue mission to bring Jack to his senses.

She wondered if his ordeal had permanently affected his personality and turned him into a hard-drinking pirate man. It didn't seem like her old Jack, wanting to run a bar for the rest of his life. This was probably a mistake she thought. I have no desire to serve food and drinks to people.

The vehicle pulled into a parking lot and up to a moderate size office building. It was a new looking building with black granite facing and four stories tall.

"This is your destination Miss Montgomery. Mr. McCabe will be waiting for you on the fourth floor."

Shelly climbed out of the limousine and proceeded into the building. The building directory by the elevator simply listed the 4th floor as McCabe Enterprises. The lobby was a sunny atmosphere with sky lights and a fountain. Green plants and large potted trees surrounded the fountain in the building foyer.

Pressing the up button, the elevator door opened. She stepped in and proceeded to floor number four. This is kind of weird she thought. Maybe this is the restaurant headquarters or something.

As the elevator door opened a group of people in wheelchairs and various prosthesis greeted her. Everyone in the room seemed to have some type of handicap. Jack was in the middle of the group and moved forward and gave her a hug.

"Hello, Shelly."

"Welcome to McCabe Enterprises. We specialize in a few different areas. One of them is helping victims of severe violent crime regain their self confidence and move on in life. We help them overcome their psychological and physical issues brought on by crime. We also have physical rehabilitation facilities are on the third floor. A psychiatrist counseling unit and job search facilities on the second floor. And the first floor has several offices dedicated to finding victims and bringing them to McCabe Enterprises for treatment and adjustment to their new conditions."

Shelly just listened in amazement as Jack continued.

"All of these people have become handicapped in some way from being a victim of crime. Just like me and you. We find a safe place for them to regroup and get them the help they need. None of the clients we accept get the kind of help we did from the FBI. It is much more of a struggle for them to get back and function in life under their new circumstances. Most get very little if any money in terms of restitution from the crime. None of the victims we help can afford fancy prosthesis devices and other equipment like we were given. Some have lost their entire families. Others have had tragic circumstances that make our situation look like a cake walk."

He continued to explain what they do.

"One guy we just recently released used crutches for five years after his leg was blown off by a shotgun in a convenience store robbery. He lost his job as a construction worker because he couldn't walk and went into financial ruin. All he was trying to do that night was get some medicine for his sick child. He was in the wrong place at the wrong time. He tried to stop the burglary and probably saved a woman's life that night in the process. He was dubbed a hero for his efforts."

"They caught the man who shot him, but the criminal was broke and didn't have a dime to his name. The store owner's insurance denied the claim because the hero got involved and tried to save the woman. Like I said, he hobbled around on crutches for five years because he was broke. Before the incident he was making decent money. Eventually his Good Samaritan effort was totally forgotten. At least until we heard about him."

Jack paused, "To make a long story short, we got him a state of the art spring loaded fake leg similar to the one you and I are wearing today. Then we retrained him for a desk job and got him placed in a decent position. He can now make a living again and take care of his family."

"I was hoping you might head this group up for me."

Astonished, Shelly took a step backward.

"What about the Peg Leg's restaurant and all that stuff?"

"That was a joke, Shelly. I didn't think you really thought I was serious sweetheart. That is just a place I go to sometimes to eat lunch."

She looked him directly in the eye and a temporary flash of anger came over her.

"A joke? You call that a joke? I almost didn't even come up here, you asshole. You can still sling the bullshit just like the old days, can't you?"

Jack winced at her mounting anger.

"But you did come up here sweetheart. I had to know you would follow me even if it was a crazy idea. This however, is not a crazy idea. It is a great idea. And you could help us make it an even a bigger success story."

He continued to sell her on the business idea.

"We have already helped many people. We get them involved in handicapped sporting events. We find them shelter and counseling. If they are under age we find foster homes for them if they need to get out of their current environment. We fight legal battles in custody court sometimes for them. We do whatever it takes to help the people who have had a crummy shake in life from being a victim of violent crime. We can't help everyone but we are making a difference for some."

"And here is the best part about it. We are subsidized by the Federal Government for helping these people. We don't have to charge the victims a dime for our efforts. All we have to do is help them and get them the services they need. What do you think? Are you in?"

A smile grew over Shelly's face as she looked at Jack with that big smile across his face. This was perfect, she thought. This must be the guy for me, getting me to come all the way up here under false pretenses. This sounds like my kind of occupation. Shelly had always wanted to help people on her job. This made perfect sense given her new physical condition.

"Yeah, I'm in Jack. You should have told me though. I would love to help these people." She changed her tone. "Wait a minute. What is that condition stuff you were emailing me about if I showed up?"

"Well that part is really straightforward and simple. It just requires a simple yes or no on your part."

Jack dropped to one knee in front of her and held her hand.

"Will you marry me and become a life long partner in McCabe Enterprises?"

Shelly laughed out loud at his humbleness.

"The answer is yes, I will, Jack. How could I resist a smile like that?"

The crowd of employees around them erupted in cheers at her response. Jack kissed her and carried her into his office. It was messy and strewn with paperwork.

"You look like you could use some organizational skills," she responded. "But how do I know you are serious and don't just need me to run this business?"

Jack rummaged around his office through several drawers. "It must be here somewhere" he said. Finally he pulled out a small ring container from the drawer and dropped to one knee again in official marriage proposal fashion.

He opened the box to reveal a sparkling diamond engagement ring. He took the ring and placed it on Shelly's left ring finger. "I love you Shelly, will you marry me?"

A tear came to Shelly's eye as she looked at the ring. "Yes, Jack. I would be honored to become Mrs. McCabe." She embraced him and kissed him passionately.

It was all history from that point on. The business grew like wild fire and many beautiful spirited people were helped through the McCabe's efforts. Jack branched off and began investigating human trafficking out of Mexico under a special FBI contract.

With his experience from the Tanner's Lake murders, he was a natural. He spent time investigating potential destination sites for these types of activities in the North Central regions of the US. He became an expert at tracking leads on disappearing women and the sale of their services on the internet. Often times a network of rich business men were involved in the buying and selling of deprived women from outside of the United States. Utilizing specialized software to trap and track these individuals internet addresses, Jack was able to gain the location of their computers.

Once he knew which Internet Service Provider they were using, he would get their actual home address from the ISP and infiltrate the private club. He would pose as a wealthy handicapped business man interested in getting involved. Normally it could take months to gain their trust. The last case involved an organized group of Russian men selling woman to the highest bidder in a worldwide market. Those sold and moved to the United States were often transported in semi trailer trucks with false cargo compartments. They were moved across the Atlantic Ocean to the USA via large ocean going freighter ships. Once in port in New York, they were loaded into the trucks via the freight docks in disguised cargo boxes. The trucks transported them into America's heartland for their final dispatch to the customers who purchased them.

Jack focused on the trucking industry and developed new standards for searching trucks for human cargo. New heat and sound sensing scanners were implemented at truck weighing stations around the country. The technology could sense human body temperature in the truck's cargo. The goal was to eliminate large trucking as a method to transport humans into various types of bondage and slavery. The new technology had resulted in a large sting operation in a trucking hub in northern Illinois. This particular ring had been moving young girls and boys under age eighteen. When the ring was busted, it secured the arrest of over twenty five individuals on kidnapping and human trafficking charges. The initial arrests helped locate several dozen children. Many of the children were runaways who had been victimized by the ring.

Drug addiction was a common method to keep kidnapped victims quiet while moving them from place to place. Several of the individuals freed from bondage were listed as open cases in missing person files around the country.

One of the individuals was a high profile abduction that gained national news coverage from six years ago. The case involved a ten year old girl who had been kidnapped on her way to a neighborhood playground. She had not been seen or heard from since the incident and was now sixteen years old.

Statements gathered on interviews with the abducted victims led to other rings outside of the United States. One young lady had been told she would be living in a mansion with other abducted girls in Germany. Her statements and descriptions of girls who had lived at the mansion lead to an investigation by the Munich police.

It was a sickening web of human bondage and suffering with captors as ruthless as any he had ever seen. Murder charges would be forthcoming on many who were involved. As ringleaders were arrested and interrogated, more and more people seemed to be involved. They came from all walks of life and many seemed like normal people on the outside. On the top levels of the ring, most were middle to upper class white collar criminals. Some of them had clean records without prior convictions. They were the type of people who kept to themselves and seemed, for the most part, to be law abiding citizens. No one suspected them, including their neighbors. It appeared that it was the kind of crime that had gone undetected for a long time.

The web of individuals involved was a very tight group and most would not talk, even under plea bargaining. The individuals who did talk helped the FBI learn how the ring operated. It also helped increase the sentences of many on the original bust.

The final delivery of the purchased individual to the paying customer was made using conversion vans under the guise of a tourist couple on vacation. The van would pull into the customer's garage and close the door. Each paying customer was required to have a locked, sound proof room built in their house to participate in the ring.

It was a sick ruthless business and putting an end to it was important. To be a part of stopping a crime of this nature felt great. Jack believed this was the most important work he had ever done. These were crimes that destroyed families and caused unimaginable suffering.

These people were not like the Griffin, an insane madman totally out of touch. These individuals were greedy, ruthless individuals who would destroy the lives of others for personal pleasure or money.

Most of them seemed to have another thing in common. The vast majority were completely sane individuals with cold calculating hearts that lacked a conscious for their heinous acts. They were actually similar to the serial killers he had studied in the past. Both criminals lacked guilt or remorse for committing terrible crimes. The main difference was the traffickers did not want to kill their victims. They viewed them as property, pure and simple, almost as if the human beings were pieces of furniture for sale. They did not seem to grasp that these victims actually had lives and families once. To them, the victims were simply vulnerable pieces of meat which enabled the traffickers to make easy money. They were modern day slave traders who could care less about the suffering.

Jack took pride that his investigative work helped gain the initial arrest and opened up the ring. Testifying in court against them was his specialty. He would use his computer generated evidence to help build the case against specific individuals.

It always amazed him that anyone could do such a terrible act as human trafficking. Usually the criminals' motivation was money or sexual perversion. The victimized individuals were often beaten, abused and forced to take drugs while in captivity. He also took special pride in helping the victims back into a semi normal life and would channel those who wanted assistance to McCabe Enterprises.

He had a staff of highly trained individuals to help them feel safe and begin recovery toward a normal life style. Most of the victims felt they could not trust anyone from their past ordeals. They all needed a great deal of nurturing in the beginning.

McCabe Enterprises had the perfect unit for helping them find their way back to society. In particular, there was one unique caring individual that headed up the department and could relate to violent crime. She had been a victim of crime once herself.

Shelly Montgomery directed a large staff dedicated to the Victims of Violent Crime. She loved her new job and was good at it. She could relate to them as a victim herself. The job was extremely gratifying for the McCabe's to be surrounded by such loving and caring people. Sometimes the victims would have the opportunity to confront the perpetrator of their crimes. Other times, that was not an option, like in Shelly and Jack's case.

Some of the victims had lost everything and had nowhere to go. Others had no family alive after whatever incident brought them to McCabe Enterprises. Those were the personal cases Shelly enjoyed taking under her wing.

McCabe Enterprises became their family. Eventually most would be placed in a family foster care environment, but almost everyone stayed in touch with Shelly. Most of them became life long friends and would contact her occasionally just like an extended family member.

It seemed that all the good in helping these people just fired more and more kindness within them. They would move on in their lives with kinder hearts, helping others in need. A snowball effect or movement started to occur which would make the world a better place someday.

Many of the young victims went from shy, scared individuals, to outgoing confident young adults. They all held a special place in Shelly's heart to see their progression. Jack enjoyed finding new clients who qualified for their subsidized services. Some of their clients went on to help others and were hired by McCabe Enterprises as staff members.

Other clients went on to become successful professionals in many different walks of life. A few became handicapped athletes and served as examples of what the human spirit was capable of achieving.

These activities ranged from down hill skiing to running marathons to wheel chair races. It was wonderful to see someone walk out their door with a new lease on life. Some were individuals who had nearly forgotten how to laugh and smile because of their tough life situations. In time, they all moved on in their lives and learned to adapt to their new world with guided counseling and support.

Time passed quickly, and their business partnership and love grew in leaps and bounds.

Exactly three years after the Tanner's Lake incident, Shelly Elizabeth Montgomery and Jack Robert McCabe were married. The ceremony took place at a little church on Tanner's Lake in northern Minnesota.

The church was filled with many people from their past, including many they had helped at McCabe Enterprises. Jack McCabe's best man was a fellow named Jason Campbell, Sheriff of Jackson County. Seems Jason had saved Jack's life on an emergency call one night. A close friendship has endured to this day. They had become fishing buddies.

Shelly Montgomery was a stunning bride as she walked down the aisle on her father's arm. Her long white gown and wedding veil contrasting with her dark hair and olive skin was a sight to behold. She was given in matrimony to her smiling husband at the top of the aisle. A beautiful ceremony was performed and the couple was joined in marriage to a tearful audience.

The reception was held at a small but friendly little place on the lake named Flanagan's Resort. It was the perfect place to start their new life together.

The End

Breinigsville, PA USA
09 April 2010

235845BV00001B/4/P

9 780982 535707